PRINCE OF
LUST

PRINCES OF SIN:
SEVEN DEADLY SINS SERIES

K. ELLE MORRISON

This novel is a work of fiction. All characters and events portrayed are products of author's imagination and used fictitiously.
Editing by Caroline Acebo
Proofreading by Norma's Nook Proofreading
Cover Designed by Cassie Chapman at Opulent Designs
Interior page design by K. Elle Morrison

Kellemorrison.com

Print ISBN: 979-8-9852047-5-9
Ebook ISBN: 979-8-9852047-4-2

DEAR READERS

This book contains material that may be considered
inappropriate for readers under the age of 18.

These materials cover:
Graphic sex between consenting adults.
Depictions of death and loss. Elements of religious
trauma,

Please leave a review ;)

To anyone who read Blood On My Name and said Sitri needed more… He got it.

BONUS SHORT STORY

Download this _FREE_ bonus short story when you sign up to the newsletter.

The events in the short story take place after _Blood On My Name_ but before _Prince Of Lust._ This short story does contain spoilers to _Blood On My Name_ so please be advised.

Kellemorrison.com

OTHER TITLES BY K. ELLE MORRISON

Blood On My Name
Audiobook:
Blood On My Name

The Princes of Sin series:
Prince Of Lust
Prince Of Greed
Prince Of Sloth
Prince Of Pride
Prince Of Gluttony
Prince Of Envy
Prince Of Wrath

The Black Banners Series:
Under The Black Banners
Dagger Of Ash & Gold

To stay up-to-date on upcoming titles, bonus material, advanced reader opportunities, and so much more visit Kellemorrison.com to join the newsletter!

For all upcoming projects and updates from K. Elle Morrison please subscribe to the _FREE_ Newsletter!

Kellemorrison.com
Linktree

I

SITRI

I tightened my grip on the back of her head. Her red lipstick-smudged mouth tightened over my cock and sucked the tip then slid back down the shaft. She was gorgeous with the trail of eyeliner and mascara running down her bright-pink cheeks. It may have taken some convincing on her part, but I throbbed in the back of her throat and groaned at the vibration when she hummed for my approval.

As the Prince of Lust, manifesting pleasure and desire in humans was as simple as existing. The taste of their sweat—of their climaxes—was the sweetest nectar. I had spilled my seed on every continent of this blasted rock more times than I could count. I breathed for the act, and being brought to the precipice by a lesser being had never lost its luster.

Until her.

Mara had been different. Not only in the fragments of her soul but in her ability to resist me. A human who captivated and excited me but did not return my adoration. I would have given her Heaven and Earth, but she was not mine to dote upon. Moving on from her had brought me more pain than I'd known before her, and in a more demented way than I cared to admit, it made my heart, soul, and lungs ache for her all the more.

A secret I would carry with me until our bones were returned to the stars.

Unlike my princely brothers, I did not carry the burden of envy or greed or a propensity for being dragged through pain and agony.

No.

I was the prince of pleasure, and if it took me five hundred years, I would return to my former glory.

If I could only reach climax without picturing Mara's face on this and every other human who became tangled in my web.

"Harder," I rasped out, flattening my palm to her head to push myself down her throat.

She coughed, and I allowed her to catch her breath before she bobbed with vigor.

My head lolled on the cushion of the couch as my cock slammed into her throat then met the back of her teeth on the upward stroke. She was working herself with her fingers to the cadence of her mouth, and the closer we edged, the heavier our breathing became.

I dug my fingers through her hair. Not to guide but encourage with a soft stroke.

Unfortunately for her, my power over her body and mind had dwindled to nothing more than flesh on flesh.

I was Prince of Lust by title alone. I'd lost all of my potency.

The moment her cunt convulsed and spasmed with her release, my hips bucked then stalled deep within her strained throat. My cocked jerked and filled her cheeks with my seed. She swallowed me down and licked the tip for every last drop with grateful laps.

When she had her fill, I cupped her jaw and brought her up to me.

"Thank you, beautiful," I said, then gave her a quick peck on the lips before roughing her chin away from me.

She straightened her dress and wiped the dark stains from her cheeks with her sodden fingers before turning toward the door without a word. Her disappointment that I hadn't asked her to stay was expected. As was the awkward look over her shoulder before she opened the door.

"Call me?" she squeaked out through bruised vocal cords.

I gave her a curt nod, and she smiled as if I'd confessed my undying love for her.

She pulled the metal door open, and the pounding bass of the club below broke through the office before she scurried out. Silence, stale booze, and sex thickened the room before a voice came from the desk behind me.

"Did you even get her number?"

Ezequiel.

No matter when he'd decided to appear, he had just gotten a decent show.

"No," I answered, getting to my feet to fasten my pants. "What is it the humans like to say? If it is meant to be, it will be."

"How little they know of fate," he mused.

I stretched my arms over my head, feeling the muscles in my back and sides prickle and pull. When my body relaxed, I looked Ezequiel over more closely. He looked haggard and was wearing the same clothing I'd seen him in two nights ago, which was the last time I'd been sober enough to realize he had left me for more than a few hours. An unusual practice since we'd become business partners all those years ago.

"What type of trouble have you just unfurled from?"

"Far more than you have lately," he said with a wiggle of his brow.

He wasn't referring to the amount of sex I was having—or the lack thereof. He'd seen firsthand that the gift that had been bestowed upon me had faded. Before, willing participants had allowed me to be the conduit for the flow of energy down their spines and into their every synapse, damning them with a high they would chase for the rest of their lives but would never catch with another human. Now, what once would have been a surge of my influence into a human was now barely an ebb of pressure.

When I didn't return with a witty remark, he continued his explanation. "I told you before I left that I was summoned by Azazel."

I didn't remember, but that wasn't his fault. It was the two bottles of whiskey I'd had for dinner that night, then the handful of pills I'd taken for breakfast the next morning.

"Right," I replied dully, not wanting to have to admit that the spiral I'd been on had come to a head and the recovery was taking its toll on my mind.

He perked a brow and glanced toward the door. "I see you've kept busy without me."

"Getting back on the horse." I raised my hand and gave a vague gesture around the room.

He grinned a cocky and unconvinced grin as he got to his feet and rounded the desk to my side. He clapped my shoulder and turned me to face the large window that looked out onto the dance floor.

"Full of human idioms this evening," he said low, leaning over to my ear. "Have you had your fill of virgins on your holiday? Or should we find a hole for you to fill downstairs?"

The last time Azazel had gathered the Watcher Angels was for a twelve-hour orgy. The leader of a cult had struck a bargain with Azazel, promising him that the women who had gathered were ripe for breeding and had been blessed as a sacrifice to the Watchers for good favor with the Father.

Azazel, cunning and ruthless since his banishment, accepted the offer, and together, the remaining Watchers had descended and ravished every last virgin until they'd been used within an inch of their lives—a pack of rabid dogs presented with fresh meat.

The cult leader, or keeper, as he called himself, raged and cursed when nine months later, not one of the women had borne a child of the divine.

"No virgins this time." Ezequiel tensed the arm that hung at my shoulders. "I was punished for my part in our last agreement. For helping you."

"What?" I snapped my eyes to his.

It wasn't Azazel's place to bestow punishment on Ezequiel, and the thought set fire to my blood. Azazel held no more power than I or Ezequiel did in his self-appointed—and rather lax—leadership of the banished Watchers.

The outrage and disdain boiled within me for my brother, my most trusted friend.

"I was buried beneath the Euphrates for two days to be reminded of my ostracism and not the complete fall from grace that you have been cursed with." His nonchalant attitude did nothing to extinguish my rage.

"I am going to tear him apart limb by limb."

Ezequiel chuckled and raked his dirty fingers through his unkempt blond curls. "There you go again with the phrases of man. I am whole, brother. It was a worthy punishment for an even worthier cause. My lost weekend and your millennium of self-inflicted torture were plenty to satisfy our Father and anyone else who comes to question the ritual we performed."

He steered me toward the door as he spoke, pacifying me but not at all relieving me of my guilt. He'd suffered alone for days on my behalf. A small voice inside of me wondered if he'd done it as a way to atone for the agony he felt he imparted onto me. He had warned me that I would suffer greatly; he'd been right. But I did not regret it in the slightest. In fact, I would have done it tenfold if it meant that a small grain of hope had been unearthed within my unholy heart.

We stood at the top of the office stairs, the music of The Deacon raging in my ears. The DJ was on their fifth hour and would be announcing last call soon. The dance floor was as full as ever with thoroughly drunk mortals and the lesser demons who had come to prey on them. The club was a haven for the Fallen and had become an integral part of our existence.

Ezequiel and I had opened the L.A. nightclub to cultivate connections within the human community. All matter of humans and demons came to fraternize under our roof, and having friends high in human society had proven to be an asset time and again. Film directors would come to scope out new talent and then strike a bargain to guarantee their projects didn't flop at the box office.

Actresses and would-be pop stars would flock to Los Angeles for a chance at the spotlight, and when given the opportunity to mingle with some of the top names in the industry here in the club, they would trade their bodies and souls for a taste of their dreams being fulfilled.

Paradise for the damned. A feast for the starved.

A throne on which I sat with grateful subjects and a never-ending cache of souls to mark and covet.

Dreams were granted here, and that reputation had made it easy for The Deacon to become the most exclusive club in all of California. It was second only to our location in New York City. But I hated the cold and was not the ward of the East, so in Southern California, I resided with Ezequiel by my side.

The stains of divine annihilation were long washed away, but there were wards around the building that needed to be cleaned. And we had moved forward with construction on the second-floor addition.

We'd added a lounge for more intimate groups to mingle. The VIP booths on the second floor each sat on a glass window that looked directly down to the dance floor. The openings had to be made from underneath but would be disguised as two-way mirrors. Unsuspecting patrons below would have no idea they were being watched unless they garnered an invitation to the VIP section.

The request for more quiet seating had been echoed by many demons. They were far too worried that they would fall through the wrong hidden door on the main floor. I couldn't blame them. The lost dimensions hidden in the walls of The Deacon wouldn't only ruin a deal, but they could trap the participants in pure darkness with only the fiercest beasts as their company.

A group of tipsy women crossed our path. The more sober of them jerked around to take a second glance at the Watcher Angel and the Prince of Lust.

Even covered in silt and revenge, Ezequiel was a trophy.

My tarnishing was not outwardly displayed, but the humans whose eyes locked on mine seemed to be able to sense the challenge they would face and decided to move on to my companion.

Rightfully so.

I was tattered and jagged, unable to use the only gifts I had been blessed with upon my crowning as the Prince of Lust.

For now.

2

EZEQUIEL

When Sitri suggested we spend the weekend before the grand opening of the VIP floor in Las Vegas, I didn't expect him to invite Orobas and Stolas to tag along. They'd been investing more time into The Deacon in the last ten years and had become regulars, but they were still expected to reign over their own domains.

In the third strip club of the night, Orobas paid the owner to allow us a private group dance with six dancers. It had taken only a small suggestion from Orobas for all of them to begin an orgy on the floor.

Stolas ignored the scene and focused on his phone. He had his own agenda for the trip to Sin City. He'd purchased a chain of dance and strip clubs and was finally in the position to merge with another wealthy club owner. The slimy human would be joining us on the next leg of the night, so Orobas was told to get his most urgent needs met before that happened. Stolas had said he needed his charismatic, witty business partner, not the chaotic Mr. Hyde who had entered the first two clubs.

"Are you finished with your puppets?" Stolas called over the top of his device.

Orobas scoffed, his head lifting from between a stripper's breasts. "If you strain any tighter, that stick up your ass is going to manifest itself into a diamond just so you grant it mercy and retrieve it."

I cocked a brow. The imagery of his odd phrase was disturbing and effective.

Stolas chuckled and pocketed his phone. They pushed each other constantly, but they were two of the most powerful men, and demons, on this plane. They'd never made a bad deal, and aside from a few dukes, they had the highest soul count to date, using their gifts and determination to dominate in every business venture they dipped their fingers into.

"You have ten minutes to play before our appointment," Stolas warned as he stood up and straightened his suit. "I'll be waiting outside. Don't make a mess, Oro."

A flash of perverse joy lit Orobas' face, and I knew it was my cue to take Stolas' lead and exit. I looked over to Sitri, whose lap was occupied by a male dancer grinding himself enthusiastically to the beat of the music. With each down beat, the dancer moaned and cursed as he brought himself closer to climax.

"I don't have to admonish you of the importance of being discreet, do I?" I asked.

"The least I can do is allow my new friend to finish," Sitri said. He stopped the man's gyrating hips and looped his fingers into the dancer's waistband to release a massive, throbbing cock. Sitri's eyes rolled up to his companion's, and an appreciative smirk lit his face. He took the member in both hands and guided it to his lips.

From behind me came the pants of pleasure and pain that Orobas was orchestrating.

For a brief moment, my cock pulsed an argument to stay and participate. But knowing Orobas, he would not stop at bringing the humans to pleasure, and I was wearing my favorite white suit.

Outside, the heat of the desert hadn't pried its grip off the masses wandering the strip. Sweaty tourists passed in groups with obnoxious plastic cups in the shape of bongs, penises, and tropical fruits. Shouts from horny bachelor parties and middle-aged mortals trying to relive their youth filled the sidewalks.

The one being who stood still was leaning against the wall of the strip club, smoking a cigar.

"Too much fun for you, Watcher?" Stolas puffed at the thick tobacco stub and grinned at me through the smoke.

"Fucking humans to death isn't the thrill I came for," I said, joining him away from the hustling bodies.

"Orobas has missed Vegas. He'd go weeks without rest while we ruled over this region," he recounted, a wistful memory in his eyes as he panned across the bright lights of the replicated monuments.

"And you? Do you miss Sin City?" I asked.

He took a long drag that lit his face in a dull red flicker. After a long pause, he let loose a practiced ring of smoke.

"It's all the same," he said, bored. "Las Vegas, L.A., New York, Paris. Every place is the same. Every human is the same. Squandering their short lives for the thrill of money and power."

It was a surprising statement coming from the Prince of Greed. I didn't think he would have seen it as a problem. It was his influence, after all, that drove men mad with that sort of power. He'd been the muse of materialism for as long as man had known currency.

"It sounds like you need a new thrill." I had no suggestion to enrich his existential melancholy, not after my stint in an underwater prison for days.

Stolas shrugged and took another puff of his cigar, releasing the cloud of smoke up into a crown over his head. It hung low in the stagnant heat until the door to the club burst open and Sitri and Orobas bounded out in laughter. Orobas' shirt and jacket hung over his arm, and his torso was covered in streaks of blood from the many fingertips that had likely begged for more even as they were taking their last breaths.

"Two minutes to spare. A new record, dear brother," Stolas said with a mocking clap of his hands.

Sitri raked his fingers through his hair at my side, and together we watched Orobas shake out his shirt and put it on before doing the same to his jacket.

"In my defense, I left a few intact." Orobas smiled with pride.

Sitri scoffed. "Finally learning some discipline. And they say you can't teach an old demon new tricks." Then he led us up the Strip to our next destination.

I followed them through casinos, bars, strip clubs, and terrible shows at Circus Circus. The weekend seemed unending between the three princes of chaos and deviancy. But through it all, Sitri retreated into himself only for brief moments, and that was enough of a reason for me to indulge him in whatever his urges guided him toward—including an orgy in our room with a bachelorette party that none of them would forget.

3

SITRI

S tolas and Orobas were my first calls. A trip to Sin City would not have been the same without the Princes of Greed and Gluttony. Several years back, they resided in Las Vegas. It suited them well until Gaap and Ipos had abandoned their thrones and I'd requested that Stolas and Orobas band together with me here in Los Angeles to manage all of our territories centrally.

The weekend was what I'd needed it to be: a blur of sex, drugs, alcohol, and numb distortion that allowed me to escape from my own thoughts. But as with all enjoyment, it came and went too fast.

When the call came in, I tumbled out of bed in a tangle of sheets and human limbs. The women from the girls' trip I had met after a poker game had been eager to please. There had been plenty of them, and with Ezequiel as my second, no one noticed that I hadn't used my cock at all. But they'd all fallen asleep drunk and satisfied nonetheless.

"Good morning, my king," I rasped, my throat strained from smoke, liquor, and pussy.

Lucifer called when he was bored or agitated. Or often both.

"My office," the silky voice on the other side demanded. "At your earliest convenience."

"Of course," I answered, but the line had cut before my second syllable.

"King?" a sleepy someone asked from my ruffled sheets. "You know a king?"

"All manner of important people know me," I mumbled and got to my feet.

I peered down at the three sets of eyes fixated on my morning wood. Though it would have been opportunistic, I didn't want to risk the wrath of Lucifer over a lackluster morning tryst.

"I need to shower," I threw over my shoulder as I headed to the bathroom door. "You should probably call your future husband. Your phone has been buzzing on the nightstand for the last hour."

There was an obvious pause between all of them, either from surprise at the shift in my attitude or at the realization of what they had all committed the night before. All but one was married or engaged, and she was currently on the second bed stroking Ezequiel's cock through the sheet. He was ignoring the entire room, bored to death of the humans he'd conquered the night before.

When her hand picked up speed, he craned his neck to whisper something egregious that made her face contort with hurt and surprise. The tears easily welled in her eyes, and her cheeks blazed red with embarrassment or anger. She dressed quickly and stormed out of the room, a few of her girlfriends running to her emotional aid.

By the time the water heated, there was silence. Ezequiel lazily checked his notifications in his bed.

He finally spoke but didn't meet my eye. "What does he want?"

"Three of his princes fucked off to Vegas for a weekend. He's either calling to place blame on me or to congratulate us on the number of souls we harvested while tearing through the Strip."

He huffed out a laugh and continued his scrolling through videos with disjointed music and several seconds of catchy conversations.

The water in Vegas was harder than it was in L.A., which left a film of soap on my skin. Normally, I would have waited to shower until I was back home, but the smell of sex would attract all sorts of mischief in Hell. The last thing I needed was an incubus trying to follow me back to The Deacon. The last time one had gotten loose, it impregnated one of our waitresses. That had been a PR nightmare.

I dressed and headed down the hall. Orobas had returned to L.A. late last night after getting far too drunk and losing his shirt to Stolas in poker. He was the most likely of us to throw such a tantrum and run home with his tail between his legs. But Stolas had taken a small party back to his room, and I didn't want to leave without informing the last of my brothers of my sudden summoning and subsequent departure.

I knocked on the door, and Stolas opened it moments later with very little clothing on.

I leaned against the frame and looked past him to the two humans still asleep in his bed. "I was wondering what sort of trouble you found. Just two? Losing your touch, darling." I cocked a brow and gave him a gloating grin.

"We can't all be blessed with the stamina to entertain a whole wedding party and then fuck them all," he said, unaware of my affliction. "Quality is sometimes more interesting than quantity."

"I don't believe you for a moment. Anyway, I have to see Lucifer then get back to The Deacon. Care to come along?" I fixed a wrinkle in my shirt.

Stolas glanced back. Though I suspected he hadn't wanted to stay the whole weekend in Las Vegas, he seemed to be debating leaving so soon.

Perhaps he had more stamina than he gave himself credit for.

Stolas cleared his throat loudly, startling the man in bed from his blissful sleep. The human looked down at the naked woman then searched for the being who had lured him there the night before. He homed in on me and Stolas at the door, and he turned a deep shade of shame.

With the grace of an elephant, he tumbled out of the bed and dropped to the floor to find his clothing.

"There's no need to be bashful," Stolas said.

The man's eyes snapped to him.

"No . . . I just. I have a conference several blocks away," he stuttered out as he slipped his slacks up his bare behind.

Wherever his underpants were, he had counted them as a lost cause.

Behind him, the woman sat up and stretched.

The sheets dropped down her full, dark curves, displaying her bare breasts and satisfied face. "Good morning, puppy."

The man avoided looking at her by finding every corner of the room, either out of respect for her naked body or out of embarrassment because the next exchange showed his true colors.

Stolas leaned down and picked up a wedding band from the floor and held it between his fingers to show the rest of us.

"You dropped this last night before you plowed into our friend, but not before you buried your face in her tits," Stolas said with a telling smirk.

The human tripped over himself to get to Stolas, who dropped the thin ring into his palm.

"She'll never know, right?" he groveled. "You promised."

"Of course, Carl. She will never know."

Carl's shoulders relaxed. "Last night was"—he looked from Stolas to the naked woman, who had moved to the foot of the bed—"incredible."

She winked at him, and he blushed from the top of his balding head down to his fingers. He pulled the rest of his clothing into his chest and scooted past Stolas and me. Before he headed into the elevator, he did his best to refuse himself one last glance at what was likely the most adventurous night he would ever have on this plane.

I laughed and shook my head at the pathetic sight, then I turned back to the remaining human.

"By chance, do you know how to tend bar?" I asked. If she was up for a wild threesome, maybe she had what it took to bartend with demons.

She giggled and brought a finger between her teeth. "Sorry. Not my specialty."

"Pity."

And it was. She was very beautiful and would have been eaten up by our more ravenous patrons.

"Give me an hour and I'll meet you at The

Deacon," Stolas said, tearing my attention from his conquest.

I arched a brow but gave him a nod before stepping into the void and reappearing in Hell.

I rarely had to wait in His Majesty's atrium to be seen. The damned who were waiting, though, all gave a relieved sigh when I bypassed them and was received immediately.

The black, polished stone of the floor, pillars, and long table glinted with the many lit chandeliers overhead. I passed by the row of chairs meant for the seventy-one high demons under Lucifer's command.

I glanced instinctively at the one that held my name. My sigil was carved into the backrest. It had been ages since I'd had to sit with our brothers to discuss the state of our exile. The days of scheming to raid the gates of Heaven were a distant memory, but when ranks were pulled, we united and were expected to thank Lucifer for the high honor of being at his side.

My feet slowed as I approached where he sat on his throne. His favorite king, Paimon, stood at his side. Through the ages, Lucifer was said to have been one of the most beautiful of all the angels. Statues had been carved from stone and marble to depict the ruler of Hell.

None had come close to his true embodiment.

Much like the serpent, he was cunning, dangerous, mysterious, beautiful—and underestimated. His tall, lean frame was topped with a crown of blond ringlets, reminding me of Ezequiel. He tied his hair back so that all focus was on his sharp cheeks and jaw. His long, straight nose had a bulb at the tip that perfectly mimicked the valley in his Cupid's bow. Dimples and smile lines framed his full, pouty lips due to his easy and magnetic humor.

He was loved and feared by all who knew him. When put in his presence, you were graced with his quick wit or became the butt end of it, and you weren't aware of which until it was too late.

The last time I had stood in this spot, I'd been on a mission from my constraining angel. I was still waiting for that shoe to drop. They always did.

"The Prince of Lust to see Your Highness." Paimon's whiny voice irked the nerve in my jaw more than usual.

Lucifer glanced over at him but didn't say a word.

I bowed my head and waited for punishment or praise.

"Sitri, your actions as of late have been those of a selfish and spoiled prince. I have decided it is time for you to take responsibility."

My head rose, and my eyes fixed on the slack expression on his face.

He wasn't angry or accusatory. I'd suspected for months that I would have to pay for what I'd done. For who I'd created.

"Of course, my supreme emperor." The words rushed off of my tongue when a wrinkle of impatience pinched his golden-brown forehead.

He surveyed me for a moment then gave an instructive nod to Paimon, who walked to a door to the far left of the room. When he returned, he brought with him a scared . . . Reaper?

"Sitri, this is Dabria." Lucifer laid a hand on her shoulder and led her to stand before me. "She is the newest appointed Reaper. You and Ezequiel have the distinct honor of assisting in training her and aiding in her successful retrieval of her first three charges."

She clung to a linen bag that I assumed held a sparse number of belongings. In her line of work, she shouldn't need things, but now that she was being shoved into my lap where I resided on Earth, she would need human items to assimilate to the environment.

Her dark-brown eyes darted between mine, and her whole body shook in fear. This wasn't how Reapers were trained. Angels of Death were responsible for breaking in and supervising Reapers. It was rare a new one was appointed. Their role in the supernatural ecosystem was inherently neutral, but vastly important. Dabria would ferry souls from the mortal plane to their final destination in Heaven, Hell, or Purgatory.

"My king, I don't—"

"You've created a mess, and this is how you will clean it up," Lucifer answered before I could clarify my question.

"Right." I had no argument.

It would have been fair to say that losing my gifts of seduction, pleasure, and sexual manipulation would have been punishment enough for falling in love with a woman who would never return my affections, but I supposed being set up for failure was also a surefire way to banish me to the lowest circle of Hell.

"Hello, Dabria." I lowered my voice and did my best impression of a being who wasn't being tied to a sinking ship.

She swallowed hard. She looked at Lucifer then back at me before she spoke with a shaky voice. "Hi, Sitri."

"If you and Ezequiel fail to assist Dabria in her duty to deliver any of the three human souls to their final destination, it'll be Purgatory duty for you and imprisonment for Ezequiel, however his overseers command it, until the sun plunges this galaxy into darkness."

Lucifer sat regally back into his throne of skulls, twisted femurs, and gilded bones. He looked satisfied with his clever match and in what would most likely be a gratifying punishment I couldn't avoid.

4

BRIA

I held the small bag of possessions tight as Sitri pulled us through the void into the human world. I'd never been among humans before and was told that Reapers appeared on Earth to collect their charges and ferry them to their final plane. It was a purpose without plaudits, but I was proud to serve my place in the universe. That was until the Archangel Michael saw my existence as the perfect opportunity to punish Lucifer and the prince who had created a new demon without consequences.

When we appeared again in a large, open room, a chill washed over me. My insides churned until foul acid rushed up my throat and released on the smooth, shiny floor.

"Take a deep breath, Dabria," Sitri said softly next to me. "The unease will pass if you breathe slow and deep. The air here is thick, dirty, and hotter than you're used to."

Every sip of this new air smelled putrid. Acidic. Virulent.

The substance retching from my throat and out of

my mouth was vile.

My knees hit solid ground, and then a pair of hands raked through my hair to pull it out of the path of the sick.

"I've got you. Deep breath."

It wasn't Sitri, but whoever was holding me was someone strong and half holy.

When he spoke again, he sounded angry, but it was directed at Sitri. "What the fuck is this?"

"This is our new infant Reaper. I'll explain later," Sitri answered from somewhere far off. "Dabria, meet Ezequiel, a Watcher Angel."

I wiped the tears from my eyes and looked back to see a man who was equally—if not more—as beautiful as Lucifer or Sitri.

My stomach leaped again, but it had nothing but air left.

Ezequiel was one of the Watchers who had left Heaven to breed human women and was punished by exile and caused the Great Flood. It was a cautionary tale of becoming too involved in the lives of humans. Not needed in my utility. Humans were just my meta-physical cargo, not my companions.

"Come now, love." Ezequiel cooed and helped me to get to my feet. "I'll take you upstairs and get you settled."

Sitri, who was pouring dark liquid into two glasses, ignored the mess I had made of his floor.

"The spare room is prepped for company," Sitri deadpanned.

"Such a generous host." Ezequiel scoffed and led me toward a darkened corner.

To my surprise, we stepped into a small, mirror-lined room. An elevator, Ezequiel explained as he pushed a button on a panel near the door. I had been made with knowledge that was relevant to collecting my charges—a vast knowledge of ways humans could possibly die paired with a general understanding of how Earth was run. But there were gaps that I would eventually fill through encounters with my charges or during my time on Earth while I waited for my charges to expire.

I was expected to live here and jump right into my work, otherwise I would be plunged into Purgatory for the rest of time. Reapers were not given second chances. We were the true neutral in human existence. No one could escape us, but we were each human's eventual fate. We welcomed them into their new journey with familiarity, comfort, and acceptance. It was what my being was made of.

Well, it was what I was meant to be made of.

At the moment, I was made of cells, organs, bones, and a very unsettling feeling in my gut that quickened at the calming strokes Ezequiel's hand was making over my back.

"It will take a couple days, but you'll get used to being solid." His voice sounded duller in the elevator.

"I don't want to get used to it." My words came out on their own before I could stop them.

He laughed, and it was possibly the most wonderful sound I'd ever heard. Deep, thick, and bubbly.

"You're really cute."

Oh, Father, that fluttering feeling is going to ruin me.

"Am I?"

I didn't choose my appearance. I merely wasn't and then a moment later, I was tangible. Aside from the morphed blob reflected in the silver elevator door, I didn't have a clue what I looked like.

"Mhmm. I'll show you when we get up to Sitri's."

And as if he'd commanded it, the door opened into a hallway with only one door to enter through.

He stepped out and looked back for me to follow. "I can't stay long, but I'll show you around and help you get settled. Sitri and I have some business to attend to before the club opens for the night."

He led me into what was a kitchen. The next area was a living room, but Ezequiel held out one of his sculpted arms to show me down the hallway.

"This is the bathroom. Once the queasy sensation subsides, you'll need to become familiar with that room."

I took a step inside. The cold floor radiated up through my bare feet, then it warmed as I stood longer. Ezequiel placed his hand on the small of my back and pointed to the mirror on the wall over a sink.

"Let's introduce you to your human form," he said.

The face looking back at me was soft. My body was rounded in the breasts and hips. I ran my hands over them, becoming acquainted with their feel and look. The thick, black curls on my head danced over my brows in bouncy rings with each movement of my head. I pulled back from my reflection and stood as tall as I could next to Ezequiel. I was much shorter than he was, at least a full foot.

He watched me with a playful smile until I'd had my fill, then continued his tour.

"On the left is Sitri's bedroom. Mine is at the end of the hall there," he said, pointing to a darkened door. "And this will be your room."

There wasn't much to the space: a bed, a window, and some random furniture that I was sure humans would find comfortable. I set my bag down on the bed and ran my fingers over the plush white bedding. The dark-colored walls made the room feel closed off but calming. I didn't mind the dark, and the window gave me a glimpse of the outside world, which was a haze of buildings lit from within against a dark-blue sky.

"I hate to ask, but what did they send you down here with?"

I looked back to Ezequiel, who was leaning against the wall with his bulging arms crossed over his chiseled chest. The thin white T-shirt he wore only accentuated the defined body underneath.

"What?" I gawked more than asked.

"In the bag?" He gestured with his chin toward the bed.

"Oh." I looked inside. "The book of rules I have to abide by, a pair of clothes, something called a toothbrush, and a couple other items to groom myself with."

"A pair of clothes?" He smiled and his brows raised. The humor danced in his blue eyes, and I swore I saw specks of bright yellow shining through them.

"Yes?" Not an answer but the only word that would come.

He looked me over and gave me a smile that somehow felt warm. The uneasy feeling in my stomach was back, but this time, it warmed through me until my cheeks burned.

"Can I see the book?" He waited for me to rummage through the bag and take out the thin guidebook.

It was white, and my name was written on it in raised gold letters.

The rules weren't as simple as one would think. I was the face of peace, but I was also the all-imposing middle ground for all beings. When a human came to their fated end, I would be by their side to take them into their final beyond. Except, I was solid now and couldn't slip from void to void to find my charges. Sitri or Ezequiel would have to transport me when the visions came over me.

I hadn't been taught how to travel through the void on my own. That task was usually done by a more experienced Reaper.

The three charges could take days or months. The internal calls to their souls would be sporadic and sudden. I would have no hand in their fate or over their ticking clocks.

Ezequiel thumbed the pages with a wrinkle on his perfect forehead. "Would you mind if I take a look through this?"

"Uh—sure."

He looked up through his thick blond lashes and gave me a bright grin that made my insides wriggle again. I looked away with heated cheeks before I made a mess of the white fur rug.

"I'm sorry to drop you here and run, but I have to go."

I believed him, but I didn't want to be left alone in this strange place.

"Wander about," he said. "Get familiar with your new home, and then I will come get you in a few hours to introduce you to The Deacon." He pushed off the wall and headed down the hall.

"You expect me to just stay here?" I called after him, but I didn't leave the room he'd deposited me into. "What if I get called for a charge?"

"Scream out my name. I'll come running." His voice trailed behind him, the door closed, and I was alone.

5

A Reaper.

Why would Lucifer choose to punish me with a true neutral being?

It wasn't only my retribution. It was Ezequiel's as well.

The answer was likely as simple as Lucifer knowing I would fail and would be sent to Purgatory until the end of time. I would be stuck on that plane with Dabria. At least the destitution wouldn't be as lonely as my existence now.

I uncorked an aged bottle of whiskey. The label had peeled off years ago, but it wasn't likely I would see another occasion to drink it. The ice in my glass sang to me as I poured the brown liquor over it and filled the glass to the brim like a degenerate. I was making imaginary wagers with myself on how swiftly I would lose my immortal life here on Earth.

One day? A week?

I finished off the whiskey in two gulps, and our new bartender eyed me with concern as I took another long swig straight from the bottle. I was well into the first half when Ezequiel came strutting from the elevator. I didn't expect him to have his head held so high with the task we had been handed.

"Is she settled in her new enclosure?" I called. My voice echoed across the empty dance floor.

"For now." He held up a small book. "Did you see this?"

"Is that the new edition of *How To Care for Your Death Angel for Dummies?*" I laughed at my own joke and squinted at the book in his hand.

"It's the rules to her existence. Imagine such parameters." He fanned the thin pages across his thumb then held it out at a page with an image that had caught his eye. It was an illustration of what humans imagined the Grim Reaper to look like: a ghastly figure with a dark cloak, a skeletal face, and a long scythe. This creature didn't look anything like Dabria, with her beautiful dark-brown skin, fully formed brown eyes, and pouty lips that concealed the skull beneath.

"She's our punishment for creating." I sighed over the pages. "As if you haven't suffered enough."

"Being your business partner and the only other being willing to stand by your side isn't suffering." He elbowed my ribs, and we both laughed.

"I do seem to be collecting outcasts, don't I?" I said, a cocky grin on my face. "First, a Watcher Angel exiled by Heaven and too vile for Hell. Now, a Reaper in solid form who would otherwise only exist between the folds of time and space. What a lucky prince I am."

"She's cute," he said, watching me closely to gauge my reaction.

He'd stopped me in my tracks, and I didn't know how to react.

It wasn't that Dabria wasn't pretty. If it were any

other time in my long existence, I would have taken her to bed without a second thought. But our devious tour in Vegas proved that even in a place where it took little to no effort for a man to find a companion for the night, my gifts were fractured.

Ezequiel had seen it for himself in our room.

Though he had fucked each of the bridesmaids thoroughly, I had only used my mouth on a few, and before that, it had taken a woman on her knees in my office several minutes to arouse me long enough to get off.

Impotence for the Prince of Lust was the worst irony and would be the highest mortification if it wasn't cured soon.

Though, babysitting a Reaper would put a damper on such attempts.

I finally formulated an answer that sounded more like justification than denial. "She's . . . a Reaper."

He cocked a smile and fixed his eyes on mine, calling me out on my sad attempt at an excuse.

"She's our Reaper. For now."

6

S unday night went as expected. Humans, demons, and lesser spirits flooded the club and vied for an invitation to any open VIP booth upstairs for the soft launch. The bouncers had already removed several rowdy frat boys for trying to push their way upstairs after a group of women they were with was granted access and they weren't.

I'd meant to bring Dabria down myself but instead sent a lesser demon from Sitri's legion to assist her. He was under strict instructions to take her to the guest closet, that Sitri kept stocked with expensive labels and a ridiculous amount of accessories, then show her how to properly walk in any footwear she chose from the rows and rows of designer heels. I often wondered if every one of the princes had a thirst for more than what their abilities implied.

I glanced over to the elevator for the tenth time, becoming concerned that Dabria was refusing to come down. There was no real reason for her to be here, but jumping headfirst into human culture would give her existence here on Earth a head start.

Sitri weaved through the crowded dance floor, turning heads as he passed many willing parties who would have done anything for him to glance in their direction.

The Deacon wasn't only our business, it was a carefully curated environment that suited him. His nature could flow, influence, and intoxicate several hundred humans all at once under the conditions we'd created. Sitri's natural gifts filled our pockets and our time, but The Deacon ensured that Lucifer was happy with the game of numbers he'd set his princes out to play. In one night, I'd seen Sitri cull hundreds of souls in the name of Hell.

When Sitri reached me, I saw the elevator doors finally open, and a large demon emerged with Dabria clinging to his arm. She looked scared at first, or maybe disgusted. But after a moment of searching the crowd, her eyes settled on me and Sitri, and her brow relaxed slightly.

The demon brought her straight to us then shook his arm to free himself from her. She found her footing and watched him wander off before looking back at us. Sitri stood in silence, but his signature bored expression was more than a little interested.

She looked beautiful. Her tight curls dusted the tops of her bare shoulders, and she was wearing a practically see-through sequined dress that hit an inch or so below her ass.

"You're stunning," I said, not ashamed that I was drooling over every curve in that dress. Very little was left to the imagination.

"Is it okay? I found it upstairs. It's shiny and it fits."

The lights from the DJ booth caught in the fabric as

they whizzed by. Sitri cleared his throat and snapped his fingers to the bartender for a round of shots.

"It's perfect. Here," Sitri said, handing her a shot glass of bright-pink liquor. "A toast to your first night on Earth."

She brought the rim up to her nose and sniffed deeply. Her face contorted into a grimace instantly.

"What is it?" She held it out in front of her as if it were poison.

"Nectar of the gods," Sitri answered with a flourish of his hand. "Would you like assistance?"

She looked puzzled. She glanced from the shot to his face twice before nodding apprehensively.

I knew what he was going to do before he did it, and I didn't bother to stop it.

I considered it an icebreaker moment.

Sitri took the shot from her hand and tipped it into his mouth, holding it in his cheeks. He wrapped an arm around her waist and around the back of her neck, then pulled her against him before he dipped her like they were dancing.

She gasped, and he lowered his lips to hers to release the liquid.

Surprised, she swallowed down the alcohol and wrapped her arms around his neck. She coughed until she was back on her own two feet.

"What is that?" She wiped her lips with the back of her hand and backed out of his hold.

"Sex in a pineapple," Sitri answered with a wide, foxy grin. "A house specialty."

"Would you like another?" I asked, holding out a renewed shot.

"Can I drink it by myself this time?"

"It would be a pity, but yes." I winked and held out the glass for her to take.

Her cheeks flushed, and she brought the rim of the glass to her lips and sipped it slowly. She was about halfway through before tipping the rest into her mouth then licking her lips.

"It's . . . sweet. But it hurts?" She looked between Sitri and me for an answer or encouragement.

"It's the alcohol. You'll get used to it." Sitri signaled to the bartender that the glasses were empty. "Come with us."

He held his elbow out to her, and I stood at her other side. Together, Sitri and I led her to the VIP floor and to a free booth in the corner: the perfect spot to watch the entire room. It was quieter upstairs, and for good reason. Sitri had wanted to create a place where humans felt more comfortable and where demons could impress any human they had their eye on. Only higher-ranking demons were permitted with high-profile humans. Those matches would yield more powerful alliances.

Sitri waited for Dabria and me to settle. "I will be back in a few minutes," he said.

I shook my head. He had explained the meeting with Lucifer and the rules of our assignment, but aside from bringing Dabria here, he hadn't spent more than a few minutes with her. I wasn't going to allow him to turn his back on her or this assignment. I couldn't lose him more than I already had.

A waiter appeared at the end of our table and smiled. I'd fucked him several weeks ago, and ever since, he'd been the most attentive employee we'd ever had.

I wished that were a more frequent occurrence, if I were being honest.

"Sitri sent over a bottle of champagne." He set down three flutes and popped the cork for us. "Is there anything else I could get for you, Ezequiel?"

"This will be fine." I dismissed him with a nod, and he took the hint graciously.

I poured Dabria a glass and slid it in front of her before pouring my own and then taking a sip.

She watched the bubbles float to the top in amazement. It was curious to see a being so involved with the human experience. I took a drink, and she watched closely then tried her own. Her nose crinkled, but she went for another, longer pull.

"I like the other drink more. This one is too alive."

I scoffed. "That's an interesting way of putting it."

"I think I'm having fun. The sound makes my insides happy."

Her smile inspired my own.

"You should be happy more often. It looks good on you."

"Are you always happy? You smile a lot." She looked at me closely, inspecting me for humor or madness.

"I choose to find life entertaining. The longer I roam Earth, the more I need to find happiness to stave off the cynicism."

"I really like when you smile at me," she said, her cheeks blazing once again.

"Are you flirting with me?" I leaned closer to her and draped my arm across the back of the booth.

"I don't know what flirting is, but if it's telling you that I'd like to touch your face, then yes." She emptied her glass.

My brow popped when a thought crossed my mind.

"Did you eat before coming downstairs?"

"Eat?"

"Food? From the kitchen."

She paused, retracing the steps that had brought her to leaning into the curve of my body in a comfortable VIP booth.

"Do you know how many ways there are to die in a kitchen?"

I couldn't help my widening grin. "For you? None."

She laughed, snorted, and slapped a hand to my chest. "You're very funny. And big." She gripped my arm.

"All right. I believe you're done for the night. Time for bed, little Reaper."

"Bed?"

"Yes. To sleep off the alcohol."

"Can I even do that?"

"We're going to find out. After some water and a sandwich."

7

E zequiel scooped me up in his arms and held me close in the elevator. I was becoming more comfortable with the small moving box, and it was especially cozy when a Watcher's chest was warm against my cheek. He smelled sweet and woody. Wisps of his bouncy, blond curls fell over his brow and framed his impossibly blue eyes.

He looked down at me, where I had been staring at all of his beautiful features, and I could swear there was a holy light somewhere behind his irises.

"Is the motion of the elevator making you feel sick?" His deep voice vibrated against the side of my face.

"No. I'm fine," I said, not taking my eyes away from his. "You're very beautiful."

The muscles in his cheek tightened and pulled his lips into a dimpled smile. A gooey, warm sensation bubbled up in my core.

"You're beautiful too." There was a shift in his tone. Was it a lie?

"Oh."

"Don't you think so?" He squinted an eye and cocked his head, his whole face asking me the question.

"I like the way I feel. I didn't have any input, but I feel lovely."

When I was made into a solid being instead of a warm, guiding presence, I wasn't given any options for what my humanoid form would look like. I liked the rich, warm color that made the copper in my eyes stand out. I hadn't realized how many sizes and heights humans came in, and my frame was shorter than most of the other women I saw in The Deacon, but my hips, belly, and breasts were full and soft.

Sitri and Ezequiel had both looked at my breasts when I'd come down in this dress, but Sitri had seemed to notice my whole body, whereas Ezequiel only looked down for a moment before finding my face again.

"Here we are," he announced when the elevator door opened up for us. "Let's get you something to eat."

He lowered me to my feet outside the hallway door so he could open it, and then he assisted me inside to the couch. The ease in his walk and his movements around the kitchen mesmerized me once again. His muscles stretched his tight shirt when he reached for items in the cabinet and when he assembled the sandwich to bring over to me.

"Here, eat this and then I'll teach you how to brush your teeth."

Having to care for a body that I didn't want or choose made me feel things: anger, annoyance, and a lot of confusion. Demons who chose to reside on Earth also had to learn how to take care of their human forms, even though they would not perish if they didn't. Grooming, eating, and sleeping were part of the Earth-bound experience. The ailments that affected humans weren't genetically compatible with divinely made bodies.

Angels would easily suffer from madness, strife, melancholy, and other mental illnesses with prolonged exposure to the human condition. Demons were immune to that. Something about their grace being tarnished and their connection to Heaven being cut so long ago. It was almost as if Earth had been made for them to roam and humans created for their wicked games.

Time would tell if I would be afflicted with the same side effects that angels experienced while I was trapped here with the gorgeous angel and demon who were entrusted with my training.

"Dabria?" Ezequiel's smooth voice brought me out of my clumsy thoughts.

"I think I like Bria. Just Bria," I answered, biting into soft bread, then something salty and smooth, followed by a crunch in the middle.

A satisfied warmth filled my chest. The amalgamation of flavors and textures felt like nothing I'd expected but encouraged a craving I had been ignoring. The noise that came from my throat caused Ezequiel to chuckle. More heat rose to my cheeks.

"Bria suits you." He reached across from where he was seated and pressed his thumb to the lower rim of my mouth. With gentle pressure, he swiped a smudge of spread that had escaped my sandwich, then brought it to his lips to suck off his skin.

Food halted on its way down to my stomach, causing me to cough and sputter.

"Here, that bread can be dry." He handed me a glass of water, and I drank it down as fast as I could.

"Sitri is a little bit of a health nut. Everything has to be organic. Pure."

The way his lips formed over that last word had that funny squirm in my core activated again.

Pure. Angelic. Like he or Sitri once were.

I supposed I was pure, but not in the same way they were. I didn't feel pure when he looked at me like that or when I was wishing I were the sandwich instead of a Reaper.

"I think I need to sleep. I feel odd," I said, putting the plate on the table next to the couch.

"Can I help you get settled? It's part of my job, after all. To train you while you're staying with us."

I swallowed down a knotted emotion that had formed at his kindness, his willingness to care for a stranger.

"Okay."

He smiled, got to his feet, then offered me his hand to help me up.

He led me down the hall to the shiny and brightly lit bathroom. I'd figured out how to use the toilet, sink, and mirror, but the other areas sprayed loud, freezing water.

Unappealing, to say the least.

"I put your toothbrush here." He took the brush from a small cup next to the sink then wet the bristles under the flow of water.

From behind me, he looked at the mirror and tipped my chin up to meet his gaze through the reflection. His golden features shone under the lights overhead. If there were two of him, I didn't think my chest could have handled the pressure.

"Open your lips and bare your teeth," he instructed, showing me two full rows of dazzling white teeth. "Like this."

I mimicked the absurd facial expression, and he made circular motions with the brush against my front teeth, still smiling at me through our reflections.

He was intently watching the practiced strokes of his hand, and though I should have been learning how to brush my teeth on my own, I couldn't look away from his face.

"Spit."

My eyes bulged.

A mischievous grin played on his perfect lips. "The toothpaste," he clarified. "Spit it into the sink."

I looked down into the sink then back at him for one last confirmation. When he nodded, I leaned over and expelled the fluid from my mouth and watched it slowly flow into the drain. Back in the mirror, Ezequiel's proud expression sent warm tingles to every one of my extremities. The alcohol had melted the feeling in my limbs after the first shot that Sitri had assisted me with. The flash of that moment sent another burst of wiggling to my insides.

Ezequiel's thumb swiped away a line of bubbly foam from my chin, which did nothing to calm me. The heat he brought from my core was becoming familiar with every brush of his skin, in the way he looked at me, and when his hips pressed into my backside.

"Ready for me to put you to bed?" he whispered into my ear, the flutter of his breath sending a shiver down my spine.

"Yes." I nodded.

I watched him for one last moment, memorizing everything that I wouldn't have been permitted to experience in any other circumstance. Suddenly, I was very grateful for whatever crime Sitri and Ezequiel had committed. Feeling Sitri's mouth and tongue coaxing my bottom lip downstairs and seeing Ezequiel look at me through his lashes now was a Heaven I had never known.

Ezequiel pressed his hand into my hip and directed me to my bedroom. I looked around, unsure of what to do next. Aware of my awkward bewilderment, I wrapped my arms around myself and felt how cool my skin was now that I wasn't standing so close to him.

"You can't sleep in that," Ezequiel said, disappearing into the hall and coming back a few moments later with a large T-shirt.

"Why can't I wear this in the bed?" I looked down at the first dress I'd picked out for my human body to wear.

"Trust me. You'll be much more comfortable in this." He stepped closer and motioned down to the shoes. "Off."

I did as he insisted, and my feet sank into the furry rug under me.

He was so tall and appealing in the clothes he was wearing. The way his broad shoulders stretched the fabric of his shirt and the way the pants formed around his firm buttocks made me feel hot under my skin.

Everything about him seemed right: the way his body felt against mine and how there seemed to be a light behind his blue eyes when he looked at me.

"Here." He held out the shirt for me to take.

"Aren't you going to help me?"

His brows raised at this, and a new sort of smile spread over his face.

Surprise, maybe?

I was still learning human facial expressions, but his affected the way my body behaved. The look he was giving me, for instance, was causing a pounding sensation between my legs and my blood to race.

"I would be honored to assist you, if you don't mind taking your clothes off in front of me." He looked me up and down, his tongue flicking out and running over his bottom lip.

"I had that other demon help me get dressed. I don't really know how to get out of this dress." I turned around and showed him where I had needed help before.

"Zippers can be tricky." His voice sounded deeper and closer behind me.

The fabric loosened as his hand pulled down the contraption that held the dress together. I let it fall to the floor and stepped out gingerly, then I laid it on the bed before turning to Ezequiel, who stood staring.

I had been flustered with the other demon's help, but the luster in Ezequiel's eyes lit a fire in my chest. "You can put your shirt on me now."

"I'm enjoying the view without it, but if you insist."

He held the thin shirt up and pulled it down my body. It felt cool and light compared to the tight dress I'd been wearing earlier. Though he was taller and bulker in frame, his shirt hugged the curves of my hips, which was where his hands lingered.

"Your fingers are so warm," I said as he caressed along the tops of my thighs, following the hemline of the fabric.

"Do they feel good?" he asked, his voice huskier than I'd heard it before.

"Yes," I answered without hesitation. "Very good."

"I've wanted to touch you all night, Bria."

"Why didn't you?"

His hooded eyes searched my face, and I realized how close he was. "I wasn't sure you'd want me to."

The pressure from his grip on my hips set my insides on fire. I'd wanted to touch Ezequiel since I saw him leaning against the doorframe when I first arrived. Selfishly, I'd been thinking about the feeling of Sitri's mouth on mine since he shared that drink with me downstairs. I knew kissing was lips on lips, and I didn't know if Sitri would consider the moment as such, but I was. His hands on my neck and back had held me so firmly and safely.

Just like Ezequiel was holding onto my waist now.

"You didn't ask." I leaned into Ezequiel's chest and tilted my head up to see him fully.

"Can I touch you"—his fingers slipped between my legs and brushed at the hair there— "here?"

My pulse pounded in my chest and in the spot his fingers were circling. I opened my mouth to agree, but his lips covered mine. A true kiss. I was sure of it this time. His lips moved and sucked at mine. The movements of his hand and tongue made my head swim, and my hips searched for him.

"More," I demanded and pulled at his bicep.

He groaned and smiled against my lips.

"Did you hear her, Sitri? She's so wet for us," Ezequiel said and turned his face to the door.

Sitri was standing in the doorway, his eyes fixed on us. His face perked with interest. "What a greedy little Reaper our Dabria is."

The sleeves of his dress shirt were rolled up, and the buttons down the front were undone to show his tight body underneath. My breath hitched at the smoldering look in his eyes as they raked over Ezequiel and me.

"Not yet. You can wait a little longer," Sitri said, a mix of amusement and hunger in his voice.

Ezequiel's fingers nudged at my entrance, spreading the wet heat he'd coaxed from me. I never knew human bodies could produce such pleasurable pressure. Sex wasn't a new concept, but I hadn't thought I would experience it for myself, and never with another gorgeous man watching.

"Sitri. Please." I wasn't sure what I was asking for, but he was.

"She's ready for you, Ezequiel. Lay her down on the bed," Sitri instructed.

Ezequiel laid me on the soft blankets, and heat rushed over my body. Sitri unzipped his pants and fisted his hardened cock but didn't join us. Ezequiel stood at the side of the bed and stripped his perfectly sculpted body of all his clothing. He was gloriously aroused. The full sight of him made my mouth water as he settled between my legs and lined himself up with my core.

I looked over to where Sitri stood, and he held my gaze as Ezequiel pushed my shirt up to expose my body. He made a line of kisses down my chest and over my breasts and hard nipples. The warmth of his tongue made my body throb.

Ezequiel's cock slowly pushed inside of me, stretching and filling me. I let out a wanton sound, and Sitri bit down on his lip and stroked himself faster. Ezequiel's hips thrust slow and deep, dragging moans and pleasure from me. I cursed and gasped Ezequiel's name as his pace picked up. The storm in my lower belly tightened. I could feel my body tense and squeeze around him.

"Are you going to come for us, Dabria? Are you

going to come all over his cock?" Sitri was breathless, and his cock jerked in his palm.

Ezequiel grunted. "Fuck, you feel so good."

"More, please," I mewled. "I need more."

Ezequiel pounded into me, and I dug my nails into his back. Sitri's eyes did not waver from mine as his hand pumped to the rhythm of Ezequiel's cock fucking me.

The sound of both of them groaning and huffing my name as they got closer to their releases had my heart pounding against my ribs. The build in my core tightened. Sitri's cock pulsed, and he slumped against the doorframe until he spilled over his knuckles.

"Come for us, Bria." Ezequiel worked me until I was screaming and electricity coursed through my blood and into every limb. "You are so beautiful when you come undone." Ezequiel's voice was rough in my ear. His hips stilled, and I could feel him emptying himself inside of me.

Ezequiel rolled to my side and scooped me next to him. His damp skin was cool against my cheek and smelled heady.

I glanced back at the door, but Sitri was gone.

We hadn't asked, but there was something in his face that said he'd wanted to join us but held himself back.

I could have lain with Ezequiel forever. His satisfied breathing lulled me into my first night of sleep, and I took the image of having them both touch me into my dreams.

8

L ast night had been unexpected, to say the least.
When I had come upstairs to check on
Dabria and Ezequiel, I wasn't surprised to find
them becoming intimate. Ezequiel rarely found anyone
unobtainable, and the way he had eye-fucked her in the
club had been clue enough that he was going to make a
move on her.

I had watched as they touched and wouldn't have
intruded if not for the invitation from him. It wasn't the
first time we had shared a lover, and wouldn't be the last,
but it had been the first time in too long that the lust in a
woman's eyes had made me erect. Though I had
brought myself to climax, there had been a pull to join
them.

I brushed the thought away and attributed it to the
novelty of fucking a Reaper. Nothing more to consider.

For the luck of the Devil, another distraction
replaced the slightly awkward morning following our
adventurous night. Ezequiel had just fixed Bria some
brunch when she stopped mid-bite and her eyes lit up
behind her eyelids. She described her vision in as much

detail as she could, but as her little instruction book stated, she would only need to step into the void to appear where her charge would meet their end.

She'd seen a gathering at a house on top of some cliffs overlooking the ocean. It wasn't until we'd dressed and appeared at the front gate a few hours later that I realized it was owned by a celebrity bachelor who frequented The Deacon.

Another unexpected surprise was seeing another prince of Hell stalking around the pool: Seere, the Prince of Wrath. If he was there for a soul, then Bria would not be the only Reaper making an appearance.

Running into Seere at this party was happenstance but a pleasant one. He had been traveling for the last year and chasing the woman who held his obsession for this lifetime.

Seere's eyes were inflamed at a woman across the patio. She was staring up at a man who hadn't taken his gaze off her breasts since he'd approached her.

"Well, Prince of Wrath, what do you have planned to resolve that situation?" I asked, pointing my chin at the couple, but his attention was fixated.

"I'd like to rip that pig's heart out through his throat, but we all know that would be terrible for my image," he said, a twisted smile on his face.

"No, we can't have that sort of PR nightmare on our heads." I took a drink from my plastic cup and looked through the crowd for Ezequiel.

The victim, or charge, as a Reaper would eloquently dub them, was around somewhere, about to commit a misstep and plummet to their death from this cliffside luxury home. Statistically, the occurrence was few and far between. The likelihood of falling off a cruise ship was higher than tripping over a cliff at a lavish party.

I hoped for Seere's sake it was the unfortunate soul who was chatting up the woman he had his claws dug into. Though, I wasn't sure if it would have been kinder to the unsuspecting moron to fall off a cliff rather than meet Wrath himself. Once again, I was torn between entertainment and duty.

To my surprise, and seemingly his, Seere met my eyes. "What are you doing here, anyway?"

"Ezequiel and I are helping a friend," I answered.

He raised his brow. "Since when do the two of you have friends?"

"Since when do you obsess over human women?" I countered.

"My answer is much less suspicious than yours would be."

I glanced around, seeing my opportunity to skirt around this particular confession. "Rain check. You're about to be very busy."

His eyes snapped away from me. "Fuck," he snarled.

"Play nice," I sang in mock warning, "and come around The Deacon this weekend. Blow off some steam, and we'll catch up, brother."

He didn't answer. The two humans he had been gawking at had disappeared into the crowd, and the urgency to inflict his might was far more seductive than chewing the fat with me.

I edged the crowded deck, looking for Ezequiel and Bria, but I didn't catch sight of a single bouncy gold or dark curl among the parade of bleached-blondes and surfer mops.

Time was running out, and it would be my head if the soul wasn't ferried.

A hand caught my wrist. Then came the drunken

voice of its owner. "Hey, aren't you the owner of The Deacon?"

The small human woman beamed up at me, her glazed eyes waiting intently for the answer.

"No," I lied and pulled my hand free.

"You look just like him!" she squealed, stepping into my path.

"I get that a lot," I deadpanned. I tried side-stepping and moving past her, but her persistence prevailed.

"I know it's you. Don't you remember? I'm the girl who gave you head behind the DJ booth like six months ago. You said it was the best blow job you've had in a century." She giggled and let out a snort.

"Doesn't sound familiar." Not as much of a lie. I'd been blown behind the DJ booth many times, and many had been great.

"Such a liar."

Her playful attitude was becoming an annoyance.

"If you'd like to jog my memory, meet me in the bathroom in five minutes," I said with a wink that made her blush brighter than the calorie-free seltzer in her hand.

"Get ready for your world to be rocked." She looked me up and down, scrunching her nose in challenge. "Again."

She bounded away in time to miss me rolling my eyes.

I finally made it to the hanging garden on the other side of the yard that overlooked the rolling hills of Los Angeles. The sun had gone down hours before the party had started, but you'd hardly be able to tell because of the light from downtown L.A.

The garden was sparse. Water was more expensive than gasoline, so the planters either stood bare or were filled with cacti. Large glass bottle art stood just about as high as I stood tall, and strung lights stretched from post to post, highlighting the effort the resident urban gardener had done based on DIY websites.

I'd almost turned back when Ezequiel rounded the corner, looking over his shoulder.

I hastened to meet him next to a blooming Joshua tree. "Where is Bria?"

He didn't have to answer. Bria came from the same direction he had, her lip clamped between her teeth and worry heavy on her brow.

"He has to be here soon, right? My vision showed him stumbling over that wall there." She pointed to a low rock wall that looked more like a step than a barrier.

"Just lie low here in the shadows and he'll show," Ezequiel said to her, then leaned his head close to mine. "She saw him taking shots with a bunch of frat guys inside. He'll be looking for a bathroom any minute."

"Fuck," I cursed under my breath.

"What did you do?" His eyes narrowed at me.

My previous distraction could very well be the entire reason we were here. I pinched the bridge of my nose, already exhausted by the manipulation of fate Ezequiel and I had caused.

"There he is," Bria said under her breath, sounding excited and terrified all at once.

Relieved and eager to get the task at hand over with, I took her by the shoulders and dipped down for our eyes to meet.

"All you have to do is stand next to him and wait for him to stumble. Then his soul will meet you once his pulse stops. It's a long and rocky fall, so it should only be a few moments."

Her eyes darted behind me and then back to my face

as I spoke, but she nodded along. She closed her eyes and reached her hands behind her head to activate her Reaper's cloak. Other humans would not be able to see her, but her charge would feel her presence and know she was there to accompany him to the next plane. Ezequiel and I wouldn't be able to go with her or the soul. Though he was surrounded by those filthy with sin, he was bound for Heaven. We were not welcome there, even in the roles we were playing today.

Bria walked steadily down the path toward the spot where she had seen her charge fall in her vision, her hips sashaying in expert rhythm as her instincts kicked in.

9

BRIA

Sitri and Ezequiel wouldn't let anything happen to jeopardize my first charge.

I knew that.

But I had come close to missing the opportunity entirely.

I hadn't realized Sitri had gotten separated from Ezequiel and me when we showed up. I was so focused on finding the soul I'd been sent to ferry that I'd rushed through the gate and into the house. Ezequiel had been attached to my arm, otherwise I may have lost him too.

Being around humans made my flesh crawl. Unknowingly, they were drawn to me. Something about my haecceity gave them a sense of calm and comfort.

That was part of my job, wasn't it? Then why did it set my teeth on edge?

My charge was coming closer. The shots of liquor he'd taken inside had clearly gone to his head. The strings of garden lights ended only several feet from the garden wall, but even with the light pollution from the city, the drop-off was pitch-black.

Sitri and Ezequiel watched from the shadows, their

faces intent on the scene playing out before them. A more seasoned Reaper should have been here, but I was a punishment. They had created a new being between them, and now they were being forced to babysit the new Reaper.

They'd likely killed hundreds—if not thousands—of humans in their time on Earth.

And now they were mother-henning me without training themselves.

I was going to fail.

Fate didn't work like this. Their place wasn't in soul guidance in the same way mine was. Angels and demons tempted or saved human souls. I just dropped them off at their intended destination. I had no stake in that game of numbers; my hands were neutral.

Ezequiel still held part of his divinity. Sitri was as demonic as they came. It would have been ideal if that balanced the scales of our situation, but it didn't work that way. Their natures didn't cancel out their meddling because they didn't have a place on this end of the equation.

My charge was a few feet away from me when he finally looked up. The glassy look in his eye said he saw me. I'd been told this would happen. The human would recognize me and what I represented. Sometimes, they would sigh in relief. Other times, they would scream and fight. But ultimately, they would all come with their Reapers hand in hand.

He took a stumbling step but righted himself with a slight sway. I held out my hand and stepped closer to the edge, leading him to his last breaths. He looked at me a moment, the alcohol thick in his veins. Understanding, or maybe just the lure of my hand, brought him two steps closer, only a foot or so from the low wall.

It would be quick.

Sitri promised the fall would be fatal within moments, and then my first charge would be ushered into His grace. The first had to be the hardest.

Another step and the charge's fingers twitched at his side, readying to reach for me.

One more, and I could hear his breathing quicken and smell the alcohol on his breath.

That was it. One more step and it'd be over.

"Oh my God, Caleb. Stop!"

The shriek pulled my charge's attention away. A young woman was running barefoot at full speed toward us.

Toward him.

She couldn't see me; I knew that. But the fear and surprise in her eyes at seeing someone she knew so close to death had shocked them both stone-cold sober. She reached him in a blink of my eyes and pulled him from the edge. Their bodies fell safely to the solid gravel of the garden.

I looked up, mortified, at Ezequiel, then at Sitri. His hands fisted in his hair with his back to me.

I looked down at Caleb and the mystery woman who had just interrupted the grand design. She pulled Caleb to his feet and hauled him back to the house. The shock had worn off, and they were both laughing awkwardly at his near-disastrous stroll in the garden.

Ezequiel scowled at Sitri, who was cursing himself.

"What happened? Who was that?" I said, finally making it within earshot of their bickering.

"Sitri stood that woman up." Ezequiel's sour tone came from a level of disappointment that I didn't know he was capable of experiencing. "When she came around the corner, she was calling for Sy—"

"You're Sy?" I turned on Sitri, his face red.

"She saw your charge and forgot all about the rendezvous she was supposed to be having in the bathroom," Ezequiel finished.

The bathroom that was supposed to have been occupied, causing my charge to go outside for a piss somewhere more private.

Fuck.

"What should I do? Go push him down some stairs?" I asked without thinking.

"No. You can't be the direct cause of the death of the human you're responsible for," Ezequiel said, reminding me of the stupid rule book.

"You have to wait for your next vision. He got lucky today, but his time is up, and you'll be waiting for his next accident to come soon." He turned to Sitri. "Come on, Prince of Lust. Your low libido has gotten you into enough trouble for one night."

10

S itri and I watched helplessly as Bria's face fell and
her charge was whisked away to safety.

I wrapped my arms around Bria's shoulders
and led her toward the front of the house. "Let's get
back to the penthouse and wait for the next vision to
come. It won't be long."

My anger for Sitri's thoughtlessness bubbled up in
my gut as we left the garden.

The party hadn't missed a beat, and why would it?
After all, no tragedy had befallen one of the guests to
pull them from their drinking and carousing.

We had to find a more secluded place to disappear
into the night, but there were humans lingering around
the many vehicles that lined the hillside road. We were
almost in the clear when the sounds of screaming and
chaos caught our attention.

A group of people came filing out to line up along
the path, each one pointing out into the darkness of the
night and holding out their cellphones to record what
had caused the commotion.

Sitri turned around and walked back up the hill to

get a better look. Bria pulled out from under my arm and ran after him with me close behind. When I reached them, I saw what had everyone gasping. Out on the glassy black ocean, lit by the moon and what seemed to be several searchlights, were what seemed to be several coast guard boats surrounding a large passenger vessel sinking into the inky fathoms.

"I can't believe it!" a sloshed voice came over the hum of onlookers. "I never get to see crazy shit like this."

Bria yanked on my hand, her eyes bulging. It didn't take long for me to realize why.

The charge that had gotten away was standing right in front of us.

My spine stiffened. Bria couldn't be responsible for her charge's death, but maybe I could be. There wasn't anything in the rules about another angel causing the demise of a human being as a form of interference. His fate had already been knocked off course; a slight alteration in the location of the fall couldn't be that awful.

I took a deep breath and adjusted my weight. One swift push and we could go home successful. But Bria stopped me.

"What are you doing!" she scolded in a harsh whisper. "We can't!"

"I—"

A scream rang through the night, followed by renewed gasps and sounds of horror from all around us. Sitri stepped closer and grabbed my arm, pulling me into the crowd and back toward the street.

I searched for Bria but didn't see her. Bodies flooded the space where we had just been standing.

Sitri faced me, his cell phone illuminating his face.

He read an incoming message then held it up for me to read.

LUCI

"You won't get away with that again. Consider this your first and last warning."

My mouth fell open.

He smirked and pocketed his phone. "She should be back in a second, then we'll use this distraction to leave without being noticed."

"Are you out of your mind?"

"Don't act as if you weren't about to do it yourself before Dabria stopped you. Her pussy must be magical if she already has you wrapped around her finger."

His words hit exactly where he intended.

She *had* stopped me. There was a chance we would have met our punishments if her charge had lived to see another sunrise, but at her request, I'd folded instantly. But it wasn't what was between her legs that had me bending to her will. Not that I could form the words that described why her being called to mine.

There was no more time to evaluate my madness. She reappeared from between the folds of time and space at our sides. Her smile was bright and thankful.

"That was incredible." She grinned from ear to ear, beaming to the point that I could have sworn she was actually glowing from the inside out.

The weight of her first charge had been lifted.

"Time to go, little Reaper," Sitri said, giving me a nod to take her with me through the void back to the penthouse.

Bria lunged into my arms, peppering my cheek with kisses and squealing with happiness.

She truly was made for her job. As mad as it sounded and felt, I was jealous that Sitri had been able to give her this much joy. It could have been me if she hadn't stopped me.

I looked around one more time before departing.

Red and blue lights now lit the road and sea. With Bria still wiggling in my arms, I stepped into the void.

II

SITRI

T he rest of the week came and went without any more visions of charges for Dabria or contact from Lucifer. Since the next weekend was the grand opening of the VIP floor, it wasn't difficult to avoid Dabria sulking around. She became bored easily, and after the first day of hanging around upstairs, she'd decided to wander around The Deacon during the last bits of preparation.

Ezequiel's fondness for her was growing daily, but their budding infatuation meant she was following him around and staying out of my way.

It was midweek when she asked what she could do to help, admitting that she wanted to keep herself busy until her next charge came through. Posing as the new manager in training was enough to keep her running around leading up to Friday.

There had been so much chaos that I'd had to stick her behind the bar the entire night refilling waters, napkins, straws, and doing countless other menial tasks.

Ezequiel was too busy entertaining our more wealthy and powerful guests to spend time with her, and by the end of the night, she was throwing a tantrum on our way back upstairs.

"Why didn't you tell me that being around human men was so disgusting?" she complained as the elevator climbed much too slowly.

I shrugged. "How was I supposed to know you didn't have a liking for men?"

"They're gross, and several pinched my backside. One of them offered me money to put his penis in my mouth. That's disgusting. Do you know what those are for?"

Ezequiel chuckled next to me, watching her face make animated expressions.

"You never know, you may like sucking dick," I said, shooting a cocky grin at Ezequiel.

She scoffed. "Not likely."

"Too bad." I wiggled my brows.

Ezequiel gave me a whack on the chest. "Don't be an ass. She may not know how to strike you with a calculated comeback, but I do," he warned, and I put my arms up in surrender.

The doors opened, and Dabria was the first to step out. She sped down the hall. She hated the uniform the employees had to wear and stripped out of the black button-up and skirt as soon as she could every night. It wasn't the worst sight to see after a long day of planning and meetings with investors.

By the time I reached the end of the hall, she was already through the shirt buttons and working on the black silk skirt. Ezequiel came up behind her to watch the show for himself, his eyes alight when she got down to a lace thong and bra.

As soon as I got the door open, he scooped her up in

his arms, eliciting a screech of laughter from her, and went down the hall to the bedroom.

I headed into the kitchen to fix a snack before heading to bed alone.

They'd shared the guest room since I'd walked in on them. Ezequiel said they hadn't had sex since then, but she was uneasy being alone all night. There was nothing on this plane that I was more certain about than the trust Ezequiel and I shared, but there was a gnawing feeling in my gut when they closed the door each night.

Dabria had fallen into her human role with ease. Aside from being uncomfortable in certain clothing, she had picked up social skills and didn't have any issues talking with patrons. Her naivete often was mistaken for flirting, which resulted in large tips and many admirers. I had half a mind to lock her away in the office and give her paperwork to file just to stop seeing human men drooling over her.

"Sitri?" Dabria's sleepy voice came from behind me.

I put down the knife I was using on a cucumber and turned around to see her standing in one of my old T-shirts. My brow raised with several questions, but the most prominent was why the sight of her in my clothing was sending a signal to my cock.

"Ezequiel told me to come out for a bottle of cherry juice. He said it would help me sleep."

"You're having trouble sleeping?"

I refused myself the satisfaction of telling her the many ways I or Ezequiel could help her fall asleep. Instead, I pulled out the small glass bottle of juice from the fridge and handed it to her.

"The pressure is starting to build again. I can feel another vision of my next charge coming through. It just isn't time yet."

"Let me know when it does," I said and bit into a slice of cucumber.

"Even if you're sleeping?"

Another peculiar question was followed by a confusing sensation.

"Yes. I have to go with you, so wake me up if it's time. My door is always open to you." A slight leap of hope that she would welcome the invitation bloomed in my chest.

"Ezequiel said you often have guests in your room." She wedged herself in the corner of the counter and waited for my answer.

I took another bite of cucumber then offered her a slice, and watched as her face lit up at the new flavor she experienced when she crunched into it.

"Not lately."

"Because of me?"

A pin could have been heard in every room.

She was partly to blame for my lack of overnight visitors, but I wasn't blaming her or the task we had been handed. Having to be ready to take her to her next charge was easier to arrange if my head wasn't between a human's thighs.

"Our situation has put a momentary pause on my usual activities, but you are my highest priority."

"I am?" She smiled up at me, and if she was getting any warm and fuzzy feelings for me, I wasn't sure whether to squash them or not.

An unhappy Reaper who held my eternal freedom was more of a worry to me than my current inability to properly fuck anyone.

"I better get to bed. Enjoy your cherry juice." I turned to leave.

"Wait." She grabbed my wrist to stop me.

Her eyes dropped to where her fingers had wrapped around me.

"Yes?" I said, stepping in close to her.

"I-I don't know if I'm asking or . . ." She wavered back and forth on her thoughts. "But . . . could you not have sex with anyone while I'm staying with you?"

Unexpectedly, I laughed.

Loudly.

"Do you know who I am?" I asked. The amusement slowly filtered from my words but left a grin on my face.

"You're a prince of Hell—"

"I am the Prince of Lust. I am the warden of the West. The most potent and powerful demon on this side of the planet because, above greed or wrath or even envy, I am the root of all sin. The mere suggestion of me can bring down empires if used viciously."

She didn't step away as my torso inched closer. Her bravery would have been her downfall under normal circumstances.

"Sitri, I don't know much about human emotions," she said, her words coming out much quicker now, "but I saw the new bartender kiss you on the cheek, and the thought of anyone touching you again makes me feel anger. You might find that silly, but being around you would be easier if you promised not to touch another human until I'm done with my training and we part ways."

In all of time, I didn't know if there had ever been a jealous or possessive Reaper, yet one stood in front of me, wearing my T-shirt and asking me to keep my dick in my pants. I was astonished and fought the onslaught of urges vying for center stage. The most severe was growing in my pants and pressing into her stomach through my jeans.

"Am I supposed to accept that you will be sleeping next to Ezequiel every night while I'm obeying your request to refrain from burying my cock in someone else?"

Her eyes darted between mine, and her mouth hung open. The worn-in shirt fit her well and showed every rapid breath she took at my own admission of possessiveness.

She had no words, but her eyes held a plea that I couldn't answer.

"I will do my best," I finally said.

She swallowed hard and nodded.

"Goodnight, Dabria."

And with that, I left her in the kitchen to relieve myself of the tension she had aroused in me.

The next day, Dabria gave me the cold shoulder. The conversation we'd had in the kitchen had sat with me all night. Ezequiel told me that she hadn't slept at all, just paced her room until she finally fell asleep from exhaustion for an hour before she had to get ready for the day. I had gone downstairs to the club's office hours before either of them. Her presence in the penthouse enveloped me, and my ears had perked at every small noise. I'd kept hoping I would catch sight of her wearing another article of my clothing.

When the club opened for the Saturday night crowd, there was all manner of demons, movie stars, supermodels, and seedy politicians. I'd made my rounds and closed several deals on the VIP floor during the first hours. Dabria, though still not speaking to me, had been within sight and had ensured I was watching each time she gave an overly friendly touch or smile to certain employees she spoke with. Whether she'd wanted to prove a point or to evoke jealousy, I refused to acknowledge the acts as anything more than bratty cries for attention.

Ezequiel joined me during one of my walks around the dance floor when a group came in and I felt a sense of gravitation toward one member. We danced and shared a tray of drinks until Ezequiel pulled me to the side. He'd been warring with his own complicated feelings for Dabria, and one of the human women in our group of new friends had been a very willing participant.

I hadn't asked Ezequiel if Dabria had given him the same request to not touch another. Their relationship was not only more intimate, but the way they understood each other was easier than anything I'd seen Ezequiel share with any other angel, demon, or even Watcher. Part of me wondered if Ezequiel running his hands over the human woman on the dance floor was a test to see if he could feel attraction for another being who wasn't Dabria.

It hadn't come to light that the young woman who'd caught my eye had been claimed by Stolas until we'd met him upstairs. The marking of the damned was present in her soul, but if it had been a lesser demon or one of a lower status, I could have easily put forth my authority. It was frowned upon, and after my most recent run-in with a human who had been claimed by another, I wasn't eager to bend the rules.

Evie was her name, and she was beautiful, but something in the way her hands clutched at my chest while we danced felt almost as if she could sense the ember of my power deep within me and was determined to draw it out. Perhaps she would have if it hadn't been for the icy stare Stolas had given me.

She and the group she had come with stormed down the stairs so quickly, I paused to listen for a fire alarm. When I caught up to her on the way out, I gave her my card before heading back up to the booth to talk to Stolas, Orobas, and Ezequiel, but Dabria stopped me at the bottom of the stairs.

"She looked like she couldn't get out of here fast enough," Dabria said, her heated scowl directed at me.

"My charm is a bit rusty. What can I say?" I shrugged and mocked my own hindrance.

"I'm done for the night. I'm going up to your apartment and going to bed." She turned without looking at me and headed toward the elevator in the far corner of the club.

I looked to the top of the stairs to see Ezequiel watching the exchange with a playful, you-better-fix-that look on his face.

I rolled my eyes and let out a long, tired breath before going after her.

The door to the two-man elevator had almost closed when I reached it. I jutted my hand out to stop it then stepped inside.

Dabria's eyes bulged in shock.

"What are you doing?" she squeaked, then flattened against the opposite wall.

She wasn't going to get away with throwing a fit without repercussions. Brats threw fits when they needed attention. Unfortunately for her, Ezequiel's attention would have been much softer than what I was about to inflict.

"You tell me, Dabria. What is it you wanted me to do about that exchange we just had?" I took a short step and raised my hands above her head to cage her between my body and the wall.

"I didn't want anything from you, Sitri. I'm just another responsibility. My shift is over, so I'm going upstairs so you can cut loose and fuck whoever you want, wherever you want." Her bottom lip pouted when she finished telling me off, and I had the urge to take it between my teeth.

"Are you giving me permission to take anyone I want, bend them over, and fuck them until they're screaming? Because I made you a promise last night, remember?"

She shifted on her feet. Her thighs weren't visible under the long skirt she wore, but I imagined there was an ache between them she was trying to hide.

"I promised you that I wouldn't touch another until you allowed it," I said low. The tension in my chest grew with every word.

"I—"

"Tell me what you wanted from me downstairs, Dabria. Did you want me to take you in my arms and kiss you breathless while everyone in the club watched?"

My cock twitched in my pants, an answer to a question I wasn't asking myself.

"I wanted . . ." She breathed then took in what I was suggesting.

"You wanted me to march you upstairs and get on my knees to beg you to forgive me for making you jealous," I stated.

Whether she knew it or not, that was what she wanted. For the first time in too long, I could feel the wave of lust coming from her.

"Jealousy, little Reaper, is not what I master. To think that your request meant anything to me was your own mistake. But the heat between your legs, that is what I command."

The elevator hummed as it climbed higher and higher, but the sound of Dabria's breathing had my heart racing. She was sweet, small, and because she wasn't human, she was durable.

"Sitri," she whispered.

"Yes, Dabria?" I leaned down and brushed my nose over hers. Our lips brushed.

"The door."

"But I haven't gotten on my knees yet."

12

BRIA

I couldn't catch my breath.

Sitri sank down to the floor, the door to the hall wide open to whoever lived in the only other apartment on this level. His eyes never left my face, but his hands smoothed down my waist, then down my thighs over the long, soft skirt.

His hands bunched the material, and the hem rose up to expose my knees.

"Sirti, please not here." I pushed his shoulders away, but he was immovable.

"Not here?" He smiled, but it felt like a threat.

The first few buttons of his shirt were usually undone, but at this angle, I could see the dark ink across his chest. His blue eyes held darker intentions, but the excitement in my stomach told me to not be frightened.

His hands cupped the backs of my thighs, and in one motion, he lifted me, wrapped my legs around his hips, and got to his feet. I flung my arms around his neck, and the next thing I knew, I was inside his apartment. He hadn't bothered to take me down the hall or through the door. He'd opted to step us through the void and into his bedroom.

"Does this room feel proper?" His deep voice rumbled against my chest, which was pressed against his.

I pulled back to look at him fully, not wanting to break this moment or for him to put me down and storm off again. So I did the one thing I'd wanted to do since my first night staying with him and Ezequiel.

I kissed him.

His lips were hard and unyielding. I hadn't had much practice in this area, but the white-hot sting of embarrassment shot through me when I pulled away to search his face for any trace of emotion. I would have taken anger if it meant he wasn't so indifferent to my attempt at connection.

I opened my mouth to apologize, but he pulled me close and reciprocated. His lips crashed over mine, and his tongue stroked and coaxed the fire in my blood. This kiss was everything I'd hoped for and more. Where Ezequiel kissed me softly and meaningfully, Sitri was desperate. Hungry. Starved and ready to consume me.

He trailed his lips over my jaw then down my chest.

"On your knees," he said gruffly and dropped me to my feet.

I looked up at him. The demanding tone came unexpectedly, but I wanted more.

He unclasped his belt then pulled the zipper down to reveal his hard, thick cock. He was bigger than Ezequiel. I worried he might be too big.

"My knees?" I whimpered.

"Now."

He took off his shirt and fisted his cock, waiting for me to obey or run. I knew if I refused, he wouldn't come after me or fault me, but I didn't want to disappoint him. I lowered myself to the floor and rolled my eyes up his body. The head of his cock was engorged, and a bead of clear liquid squeezed from the tip.

I licked my lips and opened wide and expectantly.

My lips wrapped around his shaft as he eased inside. He tasted salty, but the feel of him over my tongue and the roof of my mouth produced a satisfied hum from my throat.

He pulled back just a little, and I sucked over the ridge of his head and bobbed over it. His mouth opened and let out a ragged, hitched groan, then cursed my name.

I placed one hand on his leg and the other on the base of him to bring him farther into my mouth.

"That's a good little Reaper. Swallow down my cock like the little slut you are."

The warm nerves between my legs throbbed. I wanted all of him all at once and to hear him make those demands that sent my heart racing. The pleasure in his voice was intoxicating and luscious, and it sent a warmth through me that settled in my lower stomach. I sucked harder and took him deeper. His breath became heavier, and his knees sagged the deeper I went.

My jaw ached, but I didn't want to stop. I sucked over the head and stroked his shaft. The muscles of his stomach clenched in a show of pleasure that rolled over him with every movement of my tongue. His body reacting to me, his thick black tattoos, and the scar on his arm were sights to behold.

"Stand up," he demanded, pulling at the collar of my shirt until it was over my head.

In a feverish hurry, his lips met mine. He hooked his thumbs in the waistband of my skirt and pulled it down, leaving me in the lace set that Ezequiel had picked out for me at the beginning of the night.

Sitri took no time stripping me and leaving me bare to him. His hands roved over my hips, belly, and breasts as if he were trying to memorize me as fast as he could.

He turned me to face the bed and pushed my shoulders down so that I was resting on my forearms over the bed linens.

"I want to hear you scream, Dabria. But you'll address me as your prince. Do you understand?"

"Yes," I answered right away and received a smack on my ass.

"Yes, what?"

"Yes, my prince."

My prince.

He lined himself up with my entrance, only giving me a quick moment before pushing deep inside, drawing a gasp and a cry from my lips.

"That's a good little Reaper. You can take all of me, can't you?"

He drew out his hips then slammed back in, making my knees weak as pleasure flooded my belly. When I didn't answer fast enough, he gave my other cheek a swift swat, making me throb.

"I need all of you, my prince. Please."

He thrust deeper, harder, faster. The building pressure threatened to burst at any moment as I approached climax. His fingers gripped my hips tight, and our skin slapped together. The sound of flesh on flesh echoed around the room to join the chorus of heavy grunts, moans, and curses with every dive of his cock inside of me.

"Come for me, Reaper," he rasped out.

Another demand that my body obeyed with a shuddering crash.

"That's it," he purred. "Come undone for me."

Parts of my anatomy convulsed, tightening and then relaxing through jolts of heat and electricity. The ecstasy reached my limbs and made them weak.

"Oh fuck, my prince!"

My arms came out from under me, and I rode out the rest of my orgasm with my body limp on the bed.

His cock twitched as he pulled out of me. If he'd climaxed as well, it hadn't slowed him down like it had Ezequiel.

When my senses and strength came back to me, I rolled over and looked around for Sitri. He was standing at the bathroom sink with the water running. He'd gotten a bottle of alcohol from somewhere and was taking long pulls from it.

"Do you want to shower in here or in the guest bathroom?" he shouted over his shoulder, a coldness in his tone.

A rock of unease and confusion settled firmly in my stomach.

"I can shower by myself."

I gathered my clothes and left without saying another word.

13

SITRI

The pounding in my head mimicked the noise coming from the other side of the door. I shook my head, hoping the room would stop spinning by the time I reached the knob.

"All right!" I yelled at the soon-to-be-dead person who'd woken me up at four in the morning.

I swung the door wide open to see a face I hadn't seen in years. "Vassago?"

"Hello, brother," he said warily.

I stepped aside to allow him to pass by me, then I shut the door behind him.

"Where have you been? No one has heard from you in—"

"Fifty years. Almost fifty-one. I was trapped in a human board game."

I gaped at him. "You're kidding."

Vassago, the Prince of Envy, was thwarted for decades by cardboard. He didn't look worse for wear, considering. I'd assumed he had been shielding himself behind foreign factions, inciting World War III, but he'd been hidden from all forms of tracing. Even Eligos, the duke who was known to be the most talented seeker, couldn't dash away the cloak concealing Vass.

"I was saved and want to return the favor. But for that, I need your help," he said, holding open my refrigerator door and taking out an apple.

He took a large and vocal bite then wiped the juice from the corner of his lips. Whatever he'd come for, I had a feeling I wouldn't be able to fulfill his request. After my poor performance with Dabria, it would be close to impossible to muster any of my powers to lend to one of my brothers.

"Vass, you've been gone a long time. Things aren't the way they used to be. I am not as powerful as I once was. I will do my best, but I can't promise you the outcome you might be hoping for."

It pained me to admit.

I would do anything for another prince of Hell. Vassago had fought by my side during the Fall and had spent his time on Earth inspiring war, distraction, and rampant sins worthy of the deepest pits of Hell. To say I respected him wouldn't have been a powerful enough description. He was, in my opinion, one of the most powerful demons to have ever been. And on the occasions we had teamed up, it had only taken a snap of our fingers to demolish empires.

He looked at me with a perplexed brow and a second cheek full of fruit.

I released a sigh and circled the kitchen island to check that the hall was clear. Ezequiel and Dabria were sleeping soundly in her room once again, but the sound of voices could easily wake them.

"My influence has been lacking," I admitted, pressing my forearms on the cool marble of the countertop. I hung my head between my shoulders in shame.

"I'm waiting for a riveting explanation," he said with piqued curiosity. "And remember that I haven't had a real conversation in half a century, so spare no savory detail."

I huffed a weighted laugh, unsure of where to start.

I hadn't talked about Mara or the deal I had struck with Ezequiel to save her life only to have her walk away from me forever. My heart sank at the reminder of the last time I'd seen her and the argument we'd had. Perhaps someday I would be able to redeem myself in her eyes, but I had nothing of quality to offer as a show of my growth and atonement.

"A tale for another time. But the bottom line is that I haven't been able to perform my tried-and-true powers over others in a long time. So, unless you're wanting me to extend an invitation to one of the most exclusive clubs in L.A., I don't know what I can offer you, brother."

He cocked his head and looked me over.

I didn't doubt that I smelled like Dabria; I hadn't showered after she left. I didn't want to have to go into those details with Vass or explain that there was a Reaper in my home who was relying on me to complete her training and that Ezequiel and I both had fucked her.

What a fucking mess for him to be released into.

"I don't believe Celeste would be impressed with The Deacon," he concluded. "No offense."

"None taken." I managed a weak smile and he returned with a humored shake of his head. "You must be very grateful to Celeste to come and request a favor."

A dreamy, love-sick smirk pulled at his cheeks. He was positively smitten with this human, and that alone was impressive.

"I would bring her the moon if she wished for it. But all she wants is to fulfill a dream. My influence is powerful, but not the right kind for what I want to accomplish. I was hoping to cause a great deal of lust-filled scandal to pave the way for her to win out on her ambitions."

He tossed the core of his snack into the sink and propped the heels of his hands on the counter behind him.

"Why?" It was my turn for speculation.

He took a pause, but his doleful smile didn't fade.

"She was made for me. Every speck of her being was gathered from the reaches of the universe into a soul that has been promised and presented for my repentance."

I believed him fully. As delusional, unhinged, and manic as the notion was, Vassago had been convinced that Celeste was some sort of endowment for the years he'd been exiled.

"Then you know what she desires. You don't need my influence or help."

My statement seemed to resonate. He was pensive for a moment before a sound from down the hall broke the silence.

"Vassago?"

It was Ezequiel.

"Watcher."

Unlike other demons, Vass did not shy away from the Watcher Angels. He understood them in ways that few of us could. Though he hadn't formed a bond with any other Watcher like I had with Ezequiel, Vass had respect for their kind.

"I have to go, but you owe me a titillating story and a drink," Vass said to the room, likely realizing that if I were in some sort of trouble, I would have turned to Ezequiel.

I walked him to the door and pulled him into an embrace to breathe in a brother I wasn't sure I would ever see again. His palm thumped against my back before he pulled away then stepped through the void to continue the mission he'd set out on.

14

EZEQUIEL

Bria and Sitri hadn't said a word to each other since Saturday night.

When I had come up, she was sitting on the end of her bed in tears.

Though they wanted each other, and they both enjoyed having sex, there were things that had been left unsaid on both sides. He was allowing his feelings of iniquity to build a wall that not even I could break through. Bria, though physically showing how badly she wanted more from him, would not come out and say it. They had to be the ones to resolve the situation between them, no matter how frustrating it was to watch for the next three days.

Midweek, Bria got her second vision. Sitri was in the office working when we went to tell him so we could all leave together. She had seen a small apartment, an older man lying on a bed, and a caretaker of some sort. The time had been marked on an old radio clock on his bedside table. The faux wood and black plastic framed the red numbers 4:09 p.m.

I held Bria by the waist and Sitri held my shoulder

as we passed through the black void and appeared outside of an apartment. We looked into the window through the slightly open white-slat blinds, and it seemed that no one but Bria's charge was home.

Sitri and I stood on either side of Bria as she knocked on the old paint-chipped door.

There was no answer after several moments, and only a couple minutes remained before the charge's time was up.

Sitri held his hand over the deadbolt and twisted his wrist. The pins in the lock released, and Bria was able to open the door for us to slip inside quickly. The one-bedroom apartment was dim, dusty, and piled with old medical equipment. Oxygen tanks lined every wall of the living room, save for the spaces taken up by the TV and one reclining chair.

A wheezing, gargling cough came from the bedroom followed by a cracked voice. "Hello? Mary, is that you? I thought you weren't coming until later."

I looked at Sitri then down at Bria, who was staring at the open door to the bedroom. She glanced up at the dust-covered grandfather clock then took a deep breath before taking her first couple steps toward her waiting charge.

She glanced back and whispered, "Don't let anyone mess this up."

As commanded, I blocked the only way inside the apartment and gave her a wink. She smiled, then gave Sitri a meaningful look that he somehow understood. He gave her a dip of his chin and waited with his feet anchored to the floor and his hands clasped at his back.

Perhaps there was hope for them.

The long, intricate brass hand of the old clock ticked as Bria wandered into her charge's room.

"I've been waiting for you for a very long time." The old man's voice cracked, but he did not sound scared.

"I'm here to take you onward," Bria said. Her soft voice felt like well-worn love flowing through the air.

"Thank you, dear angel."

His last words.

A few minutes later, Bria came into the living room. She wasn't as giddy as she'd been for her first collection, but there was a satisfied glow on her face.

Sitri held out his hand for her to take then turned and led her to me.

Together, we left the now-empty vessel.

Bria was in tears when the penthouse became clear around us.

Sitri pulled her into his chest and turned to me for help.

"You did so good, Bria. He was relieved that it was his time," I said, rubbing her back in the space between Sitri's arms.

"That's not why I'm upset." She sniffed and pulled away to meet my eyes.

I thought of a couple reasons why she would be upset—one being what had happened between her and Sitri. Another possibility was the realization that there was only one more charge to collect before our time together was over forever. The pain of that fact had been wearing on me as well, but I was more familiar with great loss than she was.

There wasn't anything I could do to stop the inevitable from coming, but I could comfort her. I framed her jaw with my fingers and leaned down to kiss her. Next to me, Sitri shifted his weight, likely ready to leave us alone, but that wasn't what she needed. Bria needed both of us, and if he were to walk away, he wouldn't be the only one left with regret.

I pulled away, turning her face up toward Sitri, who didn't miss a beat and pressed his lips to hers. I pulled my shirt over my head, tossed it on the floor, and stepped behind Bria to undo the button of her jeans and kiss the nape of her neck.

Her hands got to work on the buttons of Sitri's pants, then shirt, and within minutes we were stripped down and moved to the couch. Sitri sat down and pulled Bria into his lap. She sank down onto his cock and moaned at the stretch, allowing herself to bounce and fit him comfortably. I sidled up next to her and tipped her head back to kiss her deeply as she rolled her hips over him and moaned into my mouth.

"Does he feel good, baby?" I held her hooded gaze. "You take his cock so well."

Sitri cupped her ass and rocked her faster until she was coming undone and moaning for him, chanting the phrase he had requested during their first time together.

"My prince." Her hoarse voice rang out over and over.

I watched as she came down from the high of her climax, and Sitri held her tight as he jutted his hips up. My cock throbbed in my hand, ready for her. She looked up at me, and the flush of her pleasure clung to her cheeks. She opened her mouth and took hold of my shaft to guide my cock into her mouth. I groaned as she sucked and pumped me.

"More," she moaned around me. "I need more."

She would have more than she could handle.

"Such a greedy Reaper," Sitri said, stilling their grinding and lifting her off of him.

He invited me to lie down on the couch, and he sat on the low table. "Straddle his face, let him taste you."

She did as she was told. I opened my mouth and gripped her hips to encourage her with my tongue on her clit. Her sweet, wet pussy covered my tastebuds, and I was instantly addicted. I sucked, licked, and kissed until she was gasping for air and pulsing over me.

"You look so pretty riding my face," I said, kissing the inside of her damp thigh. "Don't you think, Sitri?"

"She'd look better riding your cock," he answered, a wicked grin on his face.

I pulled Bria down until she was hovering over my dick, her pussy soaked and ready for me. Sitri got to his knees next to the couch and slipped his fingers between us to massage her clit as she rocked her hips back and forth. I could feel her getting closer again when she stopped us.

"I want you both inside of me."

Sitri got to his feet, and I opened my legs for him to put his knees down on the cushion. And like the prince of sex he was, he brought out a bottle of lube from the side table drawer. A quick squeeze of the bottle and he was readying her ass for him.

She was uncomfortable as he worked his first finger in. To ease her into it, I circled her clit with my fingers. She leaned forward onto my chest and pulsed on the head of my cock as Sitri nudged her tight ring and allowed her to accommodate the stretch before inching in farther.

I cursed as the presence of him added pressure to my dick, which was still in her tight pussy. I shifted my hips, and she moaned.

"He's so big. Please," she begged.

"You're doing so well," I gritted out, thrusting gently into her. "You said you wanted it all. You can take it."

"She is so full," Sitri added, pride brimming his thick voice. "If you want more, you have to take it. Show us how badly you need to be fucked."

Sitri's words did things to her and, admittedly, me.

She cursed and bounced on our cocks. An orgasm gripped her quickly, and she melted onto my chest in a whimpering mess.

"That's my girl." I was close to bursting. "You feel so fucking good. You can give us one more, can't you?"

She nodded, and her fingernails dug into my chest and arms.

I thrust gently at first. When Sitri's hips began to move, she moaned and whimpered. Her body was ready to shatter again. I picked up my pace to match Sitri's and wrapped my arms around her shoulders to hold her close as she tightened her legs on either side of me, building the tension to her fourth orgasm.

"You're so close," Sitri gruffed. "You don't come until I say so."

She groaned with impatience, and a smack of skin on skin startled her and me both.

She gave him the answer that pleased him: "I won't come until you tell me, my prince."

"Just a little bit more," I whispered into her ear as she breathed heavier, holding herself together. "I know, baby. I know you can take it."

She nodded between grunts of pleasure. Her pussy tightened around me, and I thrust deeper, getting closer to my own climax.

Over her shoulder, I saw the embodiment of lecherousness.

There was fire and passion in Sitri's eyes as he

brought his two lovers to the pinnacle of pleasure, and the power he drew from our racing hearts flowed around us.

This was the sight that thousands had worshiped. A god of ecstasy.

"Fuck, Sitri," I said through clenched teeth.

"Come for us, Dabria," he demanded. "Now."

I shut my eyes, unable to contain myself any longer, and emptied myself inside of her.

The squeeze of her walls sent stars to my eyes. Sitri's hips bucked as I came down. Bria screamed out his name, then mine as he finished in her ass.

Panting, spent, and covered in each other's sweat, we all lay on the couch in a puddle of relief until our limbs regained strength enough to take our Reaper to bed. Together.

15
SITRI

Friday night, Gaap showed up at The Deacon and made himself at home as if he hadn't been gone for years while the rest of us had taken up the slack.

The Prince of Sloth lived up to his name in more ways than I could count.

I'd told him to meet me in the office at midnight, and in true Gaap fashion, I had to go hunting for him down in the privacy rooms.

He was pacing the floor of my office now.

Ezequiel and Dabria stood behind me, waiting for him to explain himself. I knew the Hunter he was running from by the name Alessio De Santis. Alessio was from the Order of Exorcists and had caught up to Gaap and several others in the last few years. This Hunter was far too good at his job, and unlike Hunters before him, he had no favors to grant for leniency.

Alessio had trained under the infamous Gabriele Amorth, the last chief exorcist of the Vatican. Before his death, Amorth had slipped into madness and had taken up arms against all Earth-residing demons.

Theirs was a secret society, almost as shrouded as ours. Most humans would scoff at the thought of the modern-day church believing in such practices, brushing off a common demonic possession as mental illness or a mental break.

Much like the one my fellow prince was having in my office.

"It's been a long time, Gaap." I sighed from the plush leather chair behind my desk. "Or have you become too accustomed to your stage name, Ezra St. Croix?"

"Scoff all you want, but I haven't had to hear my true name in decades unless I wanted. You can appreciate how any name moaned just right can feel more powerful than your gifts, can't you, Prince of Lust?"

"What do you want, Gaap?" Ezequiel's gruff tone was different from his usual breezy demeanor and set my nerves on edge.

Gaap sent a lethal warning glance to Ezequiel but did not respond directly to the Watcher Angel we all knew he despised. He cleared his throat and said directly to me, "The Hunter that's been tracking me. I need your help, brother."

"Brother?" Ezequiel interjected once again. "You abandon your duties, leave every one of us behind to clean up your mess, and now that you need him, he is your brother?"

I could hear the pain behind Ezequiel's words. We were all born of the same creator, with no blood shared or womb to call home before becoming fully formed entities. When it came to what was considered "brotherly," Ezequiel was the closest I could ever compare to what the human race considered family.

"Do you really want to start comparing abdications

of duty, Watcher?" Gaap said with poison dripping from his metaphorical fangs.

"Enough." I stood, tired of the infantile bickering. "Gaap, where is the Hunter?"

"Here. In Los Angeles." Gaap crossed his arms over his chest, unable to look me or Ezequiel in the eye.

I hung my head and let out a curse. Gaap was a selfish prick for leading him directly to one of the last establishments that had a peace treaty between angels and demons. There had been somewhat of a truce between the Order and us many years ago, but that was with the understanding that if they ever caught up to one of us and found a way to keep the trail, they had full right to track us to the ends of the Earth if they felt so inclined.

Obviously, Alessio had decided that banishing the Prince of Sloth back to Hell was a conquest worth pursuing across continents and oceans.

My skull was too tight, and my temples ached from the pounding anger rushing through my veins. This was the last witch hunt I needed at my doorstep. Dabria's quests were a handful enough without the Order getting brave enough to breach the walls of The Deacon to snatch the head from one of my brothers.

I pounded a fist on the desk, a childish show of aggression, but the stress was becoming too much. I didn't hear the breaking of the glass I had been sipping on earlier, but it cut into my palm nonetheless.

Dark blood gushed over the miscellaneous papers and polished wood of my desk. I was too caught up in watching the slow flow of fluid to notice that Dabria had come to my aid. She took off her black uniform T-shirt and wrapped it tightly around my hand. I stared at the side of her beautiful face. She clenched her jaw as she cleaned what she could, then looked up at me.

Caught in a silent exchange that was more feeling than verbal expression, I reached for her cheek with my free hand and brought her temple to my lip.

"I'm fine," I assured her, bringing her eyes to meet mine once more before she finished tying off the shirt and stepped back to Ezequiel, who was waiting with one of the club's promotional sweatshirts.

He gently assisted it over her head and down her body before wrapping his arm around her once again.

"Sitri, I didn't know where else to go," Gaap said, his desperation coming through now that my cool had been lost.

"Have you completely lost your grip on reality? You lured the Hunter here to Los Angeles?" Ezequiel's anger was still gritty and deep, but he had softened his volume for Dabria.

"I knew the club would be the safest place to be for now." Gaap finally addressed Ezequiel and me together, knowing he was losing this fight by having it with only me.

"Just kill him." Dabria's sheepish voice came from behind me.

The three of us gawked at her.

I dropped my head with a forceful sigh at her inability to understand the complexity of the situation.

"If it were that simple, I would have when he cornered me in Paris," Gaap answered.

"Killing him would be seen as an act of war. Every Hunter and lesser angel would be up our asses," Ezequiel further explained and pulled her deeper into his side. "No, it's best to influence or spell him away. Not raise any flags or cause any closer inspection."

Gaap surveyed the three of us. He had a puzzled look on his face that made me believe he needed to be shuffled out before he drew too much attention to the Prince of Lust and his Watcher Angel companion sharing a Reaper.

"He's warded his skin. Not just with ink, but he scarred it with hellfire."

A Catholic priest and Hunter with hellfire-marked wards on his skin? Now, that was truly a surprise.

Dabria snorted. "That's a little overkill."

Ezequiel gave her a sideways glance. She was adopting more human phrases by the day.

"What do you expect us to do about it?" I countered. "Hide you until he grows too old to pace the threshold of The Deacon?"

Gaap ruffled his hair then hooked his fingers around the back of his neck, working out what it he could reasonably ask for.

"You'll stay in one of the spare apartments upstairs," I said finally. "We'll spread word that you've gone back to Hell. He won't retreat immediately, so make yourself at home until he gives up."

I tossed him a set of keys from the desk drawer. The tag on the metal ring read the floor and unit number.

"I'll call Eligos. Perhaps he can help," Ezequiel announced, which was an oddly insightful idea.

Eligos, a duke of Hell, was a useful being to have in our corner. He might be able to conceal Gaap and the magic signature the Hunter was following.

"You have my eternal gratitude, brother." Gaap held my gaze, the keys tightly gripped in his praying hands.

"Don't make me regret this," I warned as I rounded my desk to usher him out of my office. "You may have made a name for yourself as a rock god among the humans, but our brothers believe you to be a coward and not worthy of your title."

"Prince of Sloth returning to his throne by force. Who would have thought that day would come?" Ezequiel shouted, causing Gaap's neck to tense and my mouth to quirk a cheeky smile.

16

BRIA

"You've always been too soft on him," Ezequiel said, failing to hide any discontent toward the Prince of Sloth.

"Is this how he always behaves?" I asked both of them, not sure who would answer or if they even would.

"Gaap earned his title of prince in the battle before the Fall," Sitri answered, tired, "but he took up responsibility only until he found a way to lay it at the other princes' feet. The Prince of Pride was the first to take on Gaap's legions and territories, but when the pressure of his own gifts and those of others got to be too much, he retreated to the middle of nowhere for solitude."

"You should toss him on his ass outside and allow the Hunter to do us all a favor," Ezequiel shot back.

"He can't help himself." Sitri sighed, the burden slumping him back into his desk chair. "And I owe him my loyalty. He may have abdicated his throne, but he's come to my aide countless times."

"Keep him away from me," Ezequiel remarked, his arms across his chest and a deep wrinkle across his forehead.

"He will keep himself busy. I'll call Eli, and you won't have to give him another thought," Sitri assured Ezequiel, and it was the last they spoke of it.

The rest of the night went by slowly. The music was far too loud, the patrons too rowdy, and I didn't see Sitri or Ezequiel at all until closing. We went upstairs together and piled into my bed, where we had all been sleeping for the past few nights. It had taken some convincing to get Sitri to agree, but sex was a powerful motivator, as he'd so skillfully taught me.

I slept well until midmorning, lying between Sitri and Ezequiel for as long as I could, until the pressure in my head forced me to get up.

I knew the vision would come soon, like the two before it. But this would mean that their punishment would be done and I would go back to where I belonged. I couldn't bring myself to tell them or say the words out loud. My throat strained and tightened around the thought.

I dressed for what would likely be the last time in physical clothing and took the elevator down to the club. I figured I would make myself busy washing or sweeping until the vision broke and I would have to wake Sitri and Ezequiel to take me to the charge that would surely tear me to pieces.

But when the elevator doors opened, there was a tall, rusty-haired demon sitting at the bar.

I looked around for any other beings, holy or not,

but he was alone. His head hung between his shoulders, and the slump of his back reminded me of Sitri.

"Hello?" I called, wrapping my arms around myself.

He twisted in his seat and looked me over with a glazed expression, then returned to his drink with a dismissive huff.

"Are you looking for Sitri?"

To my growing annoyance, he didn't answer. I had come down to the club to get away from the tandem breathing of the two men I would spend the rest of time missing and longing for. And here was some scruffy, long-haired jerk ignoring me and invading my solitude.

"Listen, I don't know who you are or why you're here, but unless you start talking, you're going to have to leave," I said, trying to sound as if I had any authority and reminding myself of Sitri.

He got to his feet, standing at his full, towering height, and his gravelly voice boomed across the room. "I am Ipos, a prince of Hell."

I held my breath but refused to shrink as he stocked across the empty dance floor to stand before me. His sandy eyes blazed in dominance and indignation. Out of the princes of Hell that I'd met so far, he was by far the most intimidating. But even as my spine quaked, I did not back away.

"Well, prince of Hell, I am a Reaper, and your status means nothing to me. So, again, either tell me what you are doing here or leave."

One of his sun-bleached brows perked, and he took a step back to look me over.

"A Reaper, huh?" He folded his arms over his chest. "What would Sitri need a Reaper for?"

"I'll let him know you had questions for him when you stopped by."

I didn't owe him any sort of explanation, but more than that, I didn't know what to say about what our arrangement had turned into. Sitri, Ezequiel, and I had entered into this punishment meaning nothing to each other aside from an inconvenient pause in our lives. But there was no future for us, and whatever needs we had would go unmet.

I opened my mouth to tell him for a third time to leave when the vision of my charge flashed over me.

The world around me darkened, and a crack of pain slit my temple.

The hospital room number on a door came into my sight. The clock on the wall read 2:34, and my charge was lying in the bed with many lines and monitors surrounding it.

The fleeting immersion faded, and I was looking at a struck prince who was gawking at me like he'd seen a ghost.

Ipos took another step back and cocked his head. The gold of his eyes seemed to brighten, and when it had gone, his features softened.

"I see." He circled slowly around me before speaking again. "I see much more than you know."

Decoding cryptic messages from demonic strangers was too much for my patience. "I don't care what you see, demon. Either leave or tell me what you want."

"You have somewhere to be, right?"

My jaw snapped shut.

"I also know you need assistance getting there." He left a long silence between us, letting me absorb what he was saying. "And that you can't ask Sitri or Ezequiel this time."

"Why would you want to help me?"

"Because I have seen what would happen if you took

Sitri and Ezequiel with you, and as another warden of this plane, I can't allow that type of destruction."

He held out his hand to me and waited.

I glanced back toward the elevator door. I didn't want to leave them, but I also couldn't tell them it was time for me to go. Ipos was offering me a chance to slip away and let our last night together be our end.

What better way could there be to leave?

"Will you tell them . . . tell them . . ." I choked back tears and took a deep breath to get the last request out. "Tell them thank you."

His stern face melted. "I promise."

I laid my hand in his, and he pulled us into the void.

The sucking darkness swallowed us whole and brought us into a bright, sterile hallway. Humans bustled from room to room, and the soft beeping of machines was the backdrop for what this place often was: the end of a long illness or the result of a sudden tragedy. Hospitals were one of the only places where humans welcomed the presence of a Reaper. We could be the relief of their suffering and shepherd them toward peace.

I couldn't see much of anything from the doorway of the room we appeared in front of. It was dark with the exception of the blinking green and red lights from the monitors at the head of the bed. My charge, a middle-aged woman, was staring blankly up at the ceiling. Her chest labored with each of her last breaths.

Ipos put his hand on my shoulder and dipped down to my ear. "I'll be right out here."

He didn't need to stay, but I wondered for a moment if he was ensuring that I completed my duty.

Without another word, I crossed the room's threshold and stood at the foot of the hospital bed.

The clock above the bed read 2:30. Though she didn't move, I knew she could see and feel me. She had been given pain meds to numb the many organs that had failed during her battle with cancer. But the perception of death in the room was too hard to ignore, no matter how much medication was pumping through one's blood.

"Please," my charge wheezed.

I kneeled at the side of the bed, and her glazed eyes followed.

"Please, not yet." Her words were broken by tears and heavy breaths.

"I am here to accompany you," I explained.

"My daughter." She looked toward the door. Ipos was still in the hall. "She's coming. Please wait."

I stole another glance up at the clock, then to the door. My charge's head rolled back over to face me, tears thick in her eyes.

"She knows you love her very much," I offered, knowing all too well that lost last moments could break your heart just as much as painful goodbyes.

"Please."

Her voice cracked, and pain clenched my chest.

I wanted time to wait for her, to allow her daughter to walk in before one life was snuffed out and the other changed forever. But I had no power over fate, and her breathing was slow and shallow.

I waited for her last breath to pass over her lips.

The light from her eyes faded, and her pulse ceased.

Several noises from the machines announced the loss of life to whoever was around to hear them.

I set my hand on her chest and waited for her soul to appear at my side. It was a regrettable passing, but both of us were moving on to where we belonged.

"Mom?"

My eyes snapped to a young woman in the doorway. Surprise was written on Ipos' face.

I got to my feet and watched in horror as the young woman fixed on the empty vessel of her mother. Realization, disbelief, and grief struck her all at once as she fell to her knees.

"Mom, please. Wake up, Mom," she cried. "No, no, no. Please."

I locked on Ipos. His mess of red hair and scruffy face was blurred by tears forming in my own eyes. He stepped into the room, and I felt a tug at my hand.

My charge's soul had appeared, her glow bright and grateful.

I looked back at her daughter in time to see Ipos pull the young woman into his arms before the darkness of the void swallowed me up into the seam between space and time.

My charge and I were welcomed into the beyond and taken away from the ones we loved.

17

SITRI

S he was gone.

Ezequiel had woken up before me and searched every room for any sight of Dabria, but we both knew she was no longer on this plane. We could feel that she was no longer tangible.

We knew the time would come. One way or another, we were always going to be separated from her. There was no changing who and what we were. She had her place in the universe and so did Ezequiel and I. I just hadn't expected that she would leave me in utter despair. Not only did I lose her, but I would never get to thank her for sifting through the ashes and bringing me back to the demon I had been before I'd allowed someone to burn me.

"Don't worry about work tonight," I said, grabbing my keys to head downstairs.

"You're seriously going to open the club?" Fire blazed in Ezequiel's watery eyes.

"There's nothing we can do. You knew this was the desired result when she was placed on our shoulders."

I knew he was hurt, but I was hardly holding myself together around the giant hole in my chest. Staying locked away and allowing dread and sorrow to take hold of me wasn't going to fill me with anything but more regret.

"We have to find her. Bring her home," he said, his voice strained.

His pain was suffocating. As much as I loved Ezequiel, I always knew he had a breaking point, and I feared that he'd finally found it. I opened my mouth to speak, hoping some kind of comfort would form on my tongue, when someone knocked on the door.

"Sitri," called a familiar voice. Then a familiar face appeared when I opened it.

"Ipos," I greeted. "This isn't the best time. I've had my fill of family reunions for the millennium and have my own worries to attend to. So whatever it is you've come to ask for, I am not in the position to grant it."

"I came to speak with Ezequiel," Ipos said, glancing at the weeping angel at the kitchen island.

"He isn't available either," I said, placing myself in his line of sight to shield them both.

"I saw that when I met your Reaper downstairs," Ipos said, likely speaking of a vision he had.

"What are you saying? You know where she is?" Ezequiel said, getting to his feet.

"The price of being all-knowing is that I was an intruder in the fate of her third charge. She needed help, and I saw the outcome if the likes of you two had gone with her." Ipos shot an accusatory look at us both as if what he saw was not the reality he thought he'd prevented. "I did what needed to be done. What you wouldn't have allowed to happen."

Ezequiel took in what the Prince of Pride was saying. He knew that Ipos was too often the word of wisdom and took the brunt of fate's fickle forces on his broad shoulders. I had to assume that since Ipos was also a prince, he was able to assist Dabria without Lucifer being alerted. The job was done by her hands alone, and something like envy or elation bubbled through my dejection.

"Now. I've saved your asses, and in return, I need information about a small copper ring that has gone missing from around Lucifer's neck."

He narrowed his eyes at me.

"I don't know where it ended up," I answered truthfully. I'd been the hand, but the true thief hadn't shared where they planned to take it.

"Fine. What was its purpose?" Ipos directed this question to Ezequiel.

"I'm assuming you're asking me because you're assuming it's angelic?" he retorted.

"Something like that." Ipos shrugged.

"Depending on which of our siblings it belonged to, it could be used to heal wounds, cure illnesses, or even revive those in a deep sleep. Or it could simply be tacky jewelry."

Ipos was quiet a moment, then he nodded. "Thank you. I'll assume our debts are equal."

I gave an agreeable dip of my chin. "Yes, but I also know another debt needs to be settled. Gaap is in room 406."

"Is that so?" Ipos' deep growl of an answer sent a shiver down my spine. I would hate to have been Gaap at that moment.

"It is. And he's vulnerable. There's a Hunter on his trail."

After another moment of silence, Ipos seemed to come to a conclusion about his next course of action.

"Good luck, Sitri. I hope you all find what you're looking for," he said before turning down the hall to the elevator.

18

My chest ached. Bria was somewhere between planes, in the far corners of existence that I could not reach. If I could simply step into the void and allow it to swallow me whole for the rest of time to be with her, I would have done it the moment I'd realized she was gone. But that wasn't possible for me.

I waited until Ipos was gone before addressing Sitri.

"What do we do?"

"I don't know," he said, pinching the bridge of his nose. "I don't think there is anything we can do. She is where she was created to be. You know that."

"This can't be it. She can't be gone."

"I'm sorry." He strained for the words, and I knew he was fighting his own feelings but was too enraged to acknowledge them.

"I can't be here." I let the anger fill my lungs. "I can't look at you or be on this plane without her."

"Ezequiel." There was a request to think in his tone, but I needed to escape the gaping wound between my ribs.

Without saying another word, I left.

I stepped into the void and out too quickly to the large, round double doors of Azazel's home in Aleppo, Syria. He wouldn't be able to bring Bria back, but there was no one else for me to run to.

He answered after my third knock, wearing a peacock-blue silk robe edged with gold and bronze. There was no look of surprise on his face. As always, he played his role as leader of the Lost Sons well. He reveled in the lore that had surrounded him in multiple human religions and in the tales of our sins. We'd come to this plane to breed a new race and become gods of our own, but where the rest of us took our punishments and moved on, Azazel seemed to be in a constant state of waiting for his time to rise to greatness. That included being dressed in his gaudiest, most lavish clothing at all times.

"Ezequiel, what pain has come upon you?" he said, seeing my heart in shambles.

"I've lost someone," I answered, leaving out my request to be stricken down and put out of my misery.

"It sounds like you need someone to help you find them?"

It wasn't Azazel who said this, but someone all too familiar.

Azazel stepped aside for one of our Fallen brothers to come to the door.

"Eligos?"

"Watcher," he greeted me. "I know who you seek, and as luck would have it, one of the Angels of Death owes me a favor."

His brown eyes sparkled, and I knew I would be paying greatly, but I didn't hesitate.

"I'll give you anything."

"Yes. You will."

19

BRIA

The constant darkness of the void opened up.

The warmth of the sun through tall windows that looked out over a city I'd come to find comforting told me where I was.

But why was I there?

"Welcome back, little Reaper."

His voice hitched the breath in my lungs.

I turned to find Sitri and Ezequiel standing with me in the living room. Their faces were a mix of relief, hope, and something else. It was akin to the feeling that was welling up in my chest as I took in the sight of my two men.

"How am I here?" I fought back tears, wanting to hear every word.

"We called in a few favors, owe a few new debts, and may have to take a few lives, but the exchange was well worth it," Ezequiel admitted, opening his arms for me to leap into.

Happiness purer than I'd felt in my short existence flooded every bit of my body. With my arms wrapped around Ezequiel's neck, I kissed his cheeks, nose, then finally his lips. He was real. Solid. Mine.

He set me down, and I looked at Sitri next. I knew part of him was still reluctant, but I wasn't going to allow that to stop me from holding him close.

"Thank you for bringing me back," I said into his chest.

I breathed him in. Strength, power, and home.

"This is where you belong, Dabria. With us."

"With you?" I said, looking up into his eyes.

He leaned down and kissed me softly. "With me."

20

I t'd been months since Dabria came to live with Ezequiel and me. Though she didn't need our help with her charges any longer, Ezequiel rarely missed an opportunity to tag along. He swore to never let her go again, and he took that vow to heart. Our relationship had reached all manner of demons and angels. Dabria was a novelty, and thus fielded many questions on nights she worked at The Deacon.

Tonight, she and Ezequiel were dancing on the lower level as if they were the only two in the whole club. What some would consider puppy love I saw as a healing that none of us knew we needed.

What was supposed to have been a punishment ended up being fate's way of bringing together three souls that belonged entwined for eternity.

Dabria was given a home, comfort, and a life. Ezequiel would likely say she was the greatest love he'd ever known and the only gift he would have ever wanted. But I saw how loving her had given him freedom from his past indiscretions and rid him of the guilt from many lifetimes of regret.

As for the Prince of Lust, I was more potent, deadly, and sinful than I'd been since my rebirth after the Fall. I was renewed and fueled by the desire the three of us shared. Having Dabria at my side brought me a steady focus that brought my most wicked abilities to the surface, and they shined brighter than they had been before she'd taken hold of my heart and soul.

For the rest of time, we belonged to each other. Made better by our love and forever a unit of power that could be compared to little else.

The Watcher.

The Reaper.

And their Prince.

THE END

If you enjoyed Prince of Lust, please leave a review! The next of the Seven Deadly Sins to come to life is Stolas in Prince of Greed. Find out what happen after that trip to Las Vegas and how one hand of poker changed the heart of a demon prince.

Sex in a Pineapple

- 1 oz Silver Tequila

- 1 oz Pineapple Juice

- .5 oz Orange Liqueur

- Splash of Grenadine for color

ACKNOWLEDGMENTS

Thank you to every reader who has reached out just to say they enjoyed my work. You make this life so incredible!

A special thanks goes to Booktok for being there when I need to doom-scroll instead of editing.

I'd like to also thank my writing community which has grown since my first book was released. I am thankful for each new friend.

Thank you to my husband for always supporting everything I do, no matter how crazy or time consuming.

Made in the USA
Columbia, SC
26 September 2024

43060055R00095